It was unbelievable, yet Nik wasn't joking

"I told you my period of mourning is ended," he said, "and there is room in my house, my life, for another woman—a wife. I think the vacancy might appeal to you."

"You must be deranged." Karis's look was pitying. "I've no intention of marrying anyone ever, but you'd be the last person I'd consider as a husband." She shuddered.

After the cavalier way he'd treated her, he actually expected her to consider his offer!

Nik didn't seem the least put out by her rejection. "I have the one thing I'm now convinced will make me irresistible to you. I have your son. I have Markos."

Angela Wells left the bustling world of media marketing and advertising to marry and start a family in a suburb of London. Writing started out as a hobby, and she uses backgrounds she knows well from her many travels for her books. Her ambitions, she says, in addition to writing many more romances, are to visit Australia, pilot a light aircraft and own a word processing machine.

Books by Angela Wells

HARLEQUIN ROMANCE
2790—SWEET POISON
2844—MOROCCAN MADNESS
2903—DESPERATE REMEDY
2921—FORTUNE'S FOOL
3006—STILL TEMPTATION

Rash
Contract

Angela Wells

Harlequin Books

TORONTO • NEW YORK • LONDON
AMSTERDAM • PARIS • SYDNEY • HAMBURG
STOCKHOLM • ATHENS • TOKYO • MILAN

Original hardcover edition published in 1989
by Mills & Boon Limited

ISBN 0-373-03054-1

Harlequin Romance first edition May 1990

I have no joy of this contract to-night:
It is too rash, too unadvis'd, too sudden;
Romeo and Juliet

CHAPTER ONE

STANDING before the mirrored wall, Karis dipped her head, agile fingers fastening the intricate clasp of the emerald and diamond necklace that would have cost her a year's salary. Feeling the fastening unite, she lifted her eyes to check that the exquisite piece of jewellery was shown to its best advantage on her plain black dress—and froze, her slim graceful hands still at shoulder height as her gaze clashed with the dark, level stare of a man in the foyer.

Nik Christianides! It couldn't be! More than five years had passed since she'd last set eyes on him. How strange that she should see him again, and stranger still that he should recognise her, for surely that uncompromising stare she had intercepted declared recognition? Or perhaps he had merely thought she reminded him of someone, and had been searching his memory. After all, they had never been close, sharing nothing more than a mutual antipathy, and although he was still recognisable as the supercilious autocrat she'd once dubbed him, the intervening years had changed her from a carefree teenager to a composed and dedicated career girl, whose appearance reflected the change in her life-style.

Career girl! She emerged from her daze. What on earth was she doing, staring into mirrors as if hypnotised when she had a customer patiently waiting for her to demonstrate the effect of an extremely expensive piece of designer jewellery!

Dragging her gaze away from the still, lounging figure

7

outside the windows of the prestige jewellery boutique, she turned her attention to her customer, smiling as she asked, 'What do you think?'

'I'll take it!' The American tourist beamed her happiness, as her male companion produced a credit card.

It was only after Karis had checked their credit rating, suitably wrapped the purchase and bidden them both a pleasant farewell that she allowed herself to remember Nik Christianides. A cursory glance from her position behind the counter revealed no sign of him in the busy hotel reception area. Almost unwillingly she walked to the door to obtain a fuller view. Perhaps she'd been mistaken? No, there couldn't be two men sharing that same autocratic bearing, that proud line of head as if he'd been Crown Prince to a real monarch rather than to a Greek businessman whose only kingdom was in the world of commerce.

As her sweeping appraisal found no trace of him among the continual stream of guests and staff, Karis discovered she had been holding her breath. Now she released it in a slow stream of relief. The odds were that he hadn't recognised her, or, having done so, had decided against acknowledging the fact. She smoothed the neat line of her head where her luxuriant chestnut hair had been ruthlessly drawn to the top of her head and plaited before being wound into a neatly coiled skein.

'What's up, Karis?' Annabel, the other assistant who was sharing her morning shift, looked at her curiously. 'You look as if you've seen a ghost!'

'I thought I had,' Karis admitted with a nervous laugh. 'But if I did, I'm certain now that it hasn't come to haunt me!'

'Someone from your past?' Annabel persisted, her young face alight with interest. 'Male, I bet! Some long-lost love who stole your heart and made you uninterested in the male sex for ever after?'

Karis cast her a reproving look, well aware that her young assistant couldn't understand why she never seemed to have a social life of her own. There *was* a reason, but not the one Annabel had divined, and she wasn't prepared to elucidate it to anyone . . . ever! The sorrow which had changed her choice of career, which still coloured her attitude to life, was too dark, too deeply rooted in her heart to make it a topic of everyday conversation.

As assistant manager of the prestige boutique, Karis could have kept Annabel and her youthful fantasies at a distance, but the truth was that because of the long hours the boutique was open and the costliness of their wares, which meant customers were few but discriminating, time sometimes hung heavily on their hands, and a friendly camaraderie had built up between the two girls, while they waited for custom.

'Nothing nearly so romantic,' she responded in answer to her companion's eagerness. 'Nik Christianides wasn't even a friend. Just someone I met in Crete when I was working there as an au pair for a couple of years after leaving school.'

Just saying the name of the hotel brought back memories she would rather forget. Recollections of Elizabeth Pandoulis and her two beautiful toddlers. The days of wine and roses, Dimitri, Manolis, Markos and Yanis. Yanis . . . a lump rose unbidden to her throat and she had to fight back the tears.

Damn Nik Christianides for appearing out of the blue, a spectre from the past forcing her to look backwards to days she had no wish to remember!

'I wonder what he's doing here, then,' mused Annabel, unaware of Karis's fight to control her feelings. 'Could be just a holiday, I suppose.'

'Or a business rendezvous.' Karis busied herself by rearranging a tray of wedding rings. God forbid that Nik Christianides was staying at the Acropolis! She had no wish to further that acquaintance. An unhappy thought prompted her that if Nik was on holiday in London, Annabel's suggestion that he was a guest was more than likely. Where better for a Greek to stay than in the recently opened luxury premises of a compatriot? When her knowledge of several European languages had made her first candidate for the job, she had never thought for one moment that a spectre from the past would cross her path. Now she wished she had, because the realisation of such a possibility existing would have lessened the shock Nik's sudden appearance had caused her.

She glanced down at the gold watch on her wrist, relieved to see that it was only minutes from her lunch-break. What she needed was a cup of coffee and a few minutes by herself to get her thoughts into perspective and under control.

Richard Mansell, the manager, a smart, dapper man in his mid-fifties, was checking stock sheets in the tiny office concealed from the public by a mirrored wall. Built like a glass carousel to give optimum vision to the display of costly gems, the boutique provided little privacy for its staff. If it hadn't been for the need to provide a safe, Karis had often wondered whether the designers would have omitted an office entirely.

He looked up as Karis's attractive face appeared in his vision.

'Congratulations on selling that necklace,' he greeted her with a nod of approval. 'Your sales figures are very impressive during the six months you've been working here. I shall certainly recommend that your success is mirrored in your annual bonus, Karis.'

'Thank you, Richard.' She smiled her pleasure,

delighted more by his approval than by the promise of financial reimbursement. What she was really aiming for was to achieve manager status in her own right within the next few years. Harvey and Praxel were élite in the field of retail jewellery, and she had given herself up to the age of thirty to obtain her goal. That gave her another six years of practical selling linked to management courses to reach the required standard. With no emotional entanglements to distract her, it should be enough.

'I'm taking my lunch-break now,' she informed him pleasantly. 'There's not much activity around at the moment, and Annabel can cope by herself if you want to continue with what you're doing.'

'I've nearly finished.' He glanced up at the mirror perched high on his wall through which he could see the shop floor. 'You cut along, Karis.'

Thankfully she obeyed him, putting on her cream wool jacket with its fashionably wide shoulders and tapered outline before venturing out into the watery sunshine of a London April.

The air was crisp and the clear sky promised a warmth that had not yet materialised. Karis walked briskly in her high-heeled patent shoes, their shiny blackness matched by her gloves and stylish handbag. Leaving the main West End thoroughfare with its glitzy shops, she cut down the back streets until she came to a small sandwich bar tucked incongruously between a bank and a finance company.

She had discovered the Italian-owned shop after her promotion to the Acropolis boutique. It provided everything she needed—succulent sandwiches, splendid coffee, delicious cheesecake and comfortable if slightly cramped seating accommodation at the back. For a West End eating place, it was also very reasonable.

She ordered her meal, taking it through and finding a

vacant table. She earned an excellent salary and she had been exceptionally lucky to find living accommodation a short tube ride away, in a semi-detached house which had been converted into self-contained flatlets by the elderly owner. But by the time she had paid the rent, and maintained her small but elegant working wardrobe, she had little left over for luxuries—and they didn't include lunching at the Acropolis, as Richard Mansell inevitably did!

As she sipped her coffee thoughtfully, the unwelcome image of Nik Christianides loomed in front of her mind's eye. She had only met him three times before in her life, and yet he had managed to make an indelible mark on her memory. Possibly, she admitted ruefully to herself, because it was the first time anyone had taken an instant dislike to her on sight!

She remembered that day with embarrassing clarity. It had been June in the year of her seventeenth birthday, and she had been working for Elizabeth Pandoulis about two months and enjoying every moment of it. An English girl married to the Greek manager of the large international hotel on one of Crete's northern pleasure beaches, Elizabeth had dearly wanted a compatriot to act as nanny/companion in her household, and she was more like a friend than an employer to her young au pair, encouraging the younger girl in her efforts to learn colloquial Greek so that she could eventually achieve her ambition of becoming a travel courier.

Karis sighed, forking her cheesecake with little interest, her mind too occupied with the past. That day her two small charges had enjoyed a busy morning on the beach and had fallen asleep on their beds after a late lunch. As Elizabeth was entertaining in the hotel dining-room, Karis had been alone in the penthouse apartment with its wide, secluded balcony, and had taken the opportunity of sunbathing wearing only the tiny briefs of her bikini.

Stretched out on a sun-bed, her fair skin moistened with sun-foam, her rich chestnut hair with its deep golden glints falling in an unruly cascade over the raised base, she had been aroused from a light slumber by the sound of footsteps.

Jerking upright, her first thought the children's safety, she had stared in horror at the dark bulk of the male intruder whose steady brown eyes regarded her with cool appraisal.

'Who the heck are you?' she had demanded angrily, her semi-nudity forgotten in her fright. 'And what do you think you're doing here? These are private apartments!'

'Indeed?' The interloper had been coldly unperturbed, as his eyes dwelt thoughtfully on her half-naked form. 'I could ask you the same question. When Kyria Pandoulis gave me her keys so I could collect the handbag she'd forgotten, she gave me to understand the apartment would be empty. Can it be that Kyrios Pandoulis is so under-occupied in his role of manager, husband and father that he finds time for more frivolous pursuits . . . or,' there had been a cold distaste on the hard classic features that showed no sign of humour, 'perhaps the efficient Kyrios Pandoulis has discovered a way of making his foreign guests more welcome than his superiors demand, hmm?'

Frustratingly aware that her bikini top was yards away in her own room, Karis had fought down the urge to cover her breasts. She was doing nothing wrong and she had nothing to explain or apologise for. He was the trespasser, not she! Elizabeth must have thought she and the children were still on the beach, when she had handed over the key.

'Your insinuations are insulting!' she had flared back at him. 'Both to me and my employers. Have you never seen a girl sunbathing before?'

'I have never seen a girl quite like you before, no.' The very calmness of the considered reply inflamed her, her anger overriding the embarrassment she would have suffered if he had been less aggravating.

Uttering an expression of disgust, she had risen to her feet, conscious that his eyes had never once travelled from her. Even then, amid all her confusion, she had been aware that the look was neither impertinent nor lascivious. This tall stranger was looking at her as if . . . as if she'd been nothing more than a piece of carved stone at an archaeological site. He was assessing and remote, and she received the impression that he didn't care much for what he saw.

'Do you have a name?' she had asked, matching his impertinence as she brushed past him, gathering a light wrap from behind the door and covering herself with unhurried detachment, although her fingers were trembling so much she could hardly fasten the sash. 'And some means of identification?'

'Is that necessary?' He had moved into the room behind her and now she could see his face clearly, its expression intolerant beneath the thick cap of glossy black hair that clung so disarmingly to his scalp. He wasn't as old as she had originally thought, judging him on height and stature alone as he had stood silhouetted against the sun. Probably only about ten years older than she. Certainly young enough not to be shocked by the sight of a sunbathing girl—heaven knew, the hotel swimming pool was surrounded by them!

'If you expect me to hand over Elizabeth's handbag to you, most certainly!' She had faced him boldly, edging towards where the phone was. If he had Elizabeth's keys, the odds were he was authentic. She didn't want to offend her employer, but on the other hand, suppose her employer had dropped her keys?

Hiding her indecision, she watched the flash of annoyance bring a sparkle to his eyes, as his mouth thinned in irritation. If he hadn't been so darned supercilious he would have been a very attractive man, some part of her brain registered as she waited for his next move. One thing was for sure—he didn't like having to justify either himself or his presence to her.

'I'm waiting!' she had reminded him sharply, taking two further steps towards the phone just in case, taking a malicious amusement in provoking him.

The broad shoulders shrugged, then he was reaching inside his light jacket to produce a gold case from which he took a slim white card, presenting it to her with a slight bow.

'My name is Nikolaos Christianides, and I'm on the board of management of this hotel group.'

'Oh!' Reluctantly Karis had moved close enough to accept the card, one glance confirming what he had said. She hadn't expected him to be such a big fish, and she experienced a wave of relief that she was privately employed by the Pandoulises and wasn't therefore directly answerable to his stern puritanism. She was aware that some Greek men had strong objections to their womenfolk displaying their charms so fully in public. Spyros Pandoulis for one would never have countenanced Elizabeth sunbathing with so little on, but then she, Karis, was innocent on both counts. In the first place she belonged to no Greek, and the second place she had considered herself to be private! Let him complain about her if he dared!

'Very well . . .' She had made a negligent movement with her shoulders. 'I expect Elibabeth left it in her own bedroom.' Not waiting for him to speak, she'd hurried through the adjacent door, returning with the white shoulder bag that was Elizabeth's constant companion.

Nik had taken it from her with a formal nod of thanks. 'I wasn't aware the Pandoulises had taken on personal staff?'

Presumably he was entitled to know, and any lack of co-operation on her part might go down ill for her employers.

'Elizabeth wanted someone to help her with the children, and I was anxious to learn Greek,' she informed him calmly. 'I've only been here about eight weeks.'

'That would explain quite a lot.' A mocking smile twisted his mouth as he mimicked her earlier rudeness. 'Do you have a name?'

At a loss to understand the odd disturbing current of antagonism that swirled between them, Karis felt the warm blood colour her cheeks. Pride forbidding her to hang her head, she met his dark gaze with her clear turquoise eyes. 'Karis—my name is Karis Leeman.'

'You're very young, Thespinis Leeman,' he had returned coolly. 'And you've still got a lot to learn about life. Let me give you at least one piece of advice . . .'

He had paused, and she'd held herself stiffly, expecting some lecture about her manners or her behaviour.

'Your pale northern skin has taken as much of our southern sun as it can cope with today. Ignore my advice if you will, but it would be a pity to burn such virgin flesh.'

It had been said with a cold impersonality that was totally inoffensive, and she had watched him leave with mixed feelings about his intrusion.

Elizabeth had been full of apologies when she had returned an hour later.

'How stupid of me!' she'd castigated herself. 'I clean forgot you and the chidren would be there, but you know what I'm like without my bag . . .. So when Nik offered to fetch it, I just handed over the key. I really am dreadfully sorry, Karis, if you were distressed.'

'Not really,' Karis had lied. 'I'm afraid his attitude riled me a bit. It was as if he'd never seen a woman topless before. To be honest, I thought he was a—a supercilious autocrat!'

Elizabeth had been unable to contain her amusement. 'What a marvellous description!' she had declared. 'But grossly unfair if you really knew Nik. And as for his never having seen a naked woman before, you're quite wrong there. Nik has been married to his childhood sweetheart for the last six years. A more loving and devoted couple I've yet to see, so I don't imagine he's deprived of intimacies far more revealing than a topless tourist . . .'

Staring down at the remains of the cheesecake, Karis was astonished to find that she had reduced it to inedible crumbs. Well, she hadn't been feeling very hungry anyway, she decided, rising to her feet, and making for the exit.

Taking her time, she strolled back to the fashionable shopping centre enjoying the pale warmth of the sun on her face, pausing to window-shop in an effort to live in the present.

Eventually she was forced to admit that seeing Nik Christianides had awakened carefully preserved yet dormant memories that refused to be pushed back into oblivion.

Strange that Nik should be the catalyst. She had lived in Crete for two years and had only seen him on two further occasions—both disquieting. The first had been a year after their first encounter when he paid a routine visit to the hotel and insisted on entertaining the Pandoulises at his own expense, and Karis had been obliged to spend the day in his company in her role of nanny to the children. It had been a strange, tension-filled day, leaving her with the impression that, although she had been invited, her presence had been resented by her host.

The third and last time had been the following Christmas.

The hotel had staged a Christmas party for its winter visitors and she had joined them for the celebration evening dinner in the beautifully decorated hotel dining-room. She had been late in arriving, self-conscious in the new dress Elizabeth had insisted on buying for her. The first person she had seen was Nik Christianides. Their eyes had clashed across the room, a spark of recognition igniting, then Nik's gaze had drifted downwards, leaving her face to linger on the unmistakable swell of her body which even the pretty maternity dress could not diguise.

This time she had been unable to meet his contemptuous appraisal. Turning abruptly she'd run from the room, not stopping until she'd gained the sanctuary of her own bedroom. There she had sat on her bed, cradling her unborn child. An orphan even before he saw the light of day. Something had told her that the child would be a boy, that Yanís, whom she had loved so desperately, would father a son. . .

She was nearly at the Acropolis now, her subconscious mind guiding her footsteps, as, head down, mouth tightly compressed, she relived the past. She had been right. The baby she had borne in February had been a boy. Markos . . . Despite what had happened she had called him Markos after Yanís's father in the time-honoured custom, and for a few brief weeks she'd lavished all her love and attention on him. Then she had lost him, and the pain had been so bad she thought she was going to die. Because that mercy hadn't been granted her, she had had to learn to cope with life without him. On the surface she'd been very successful. No one knew the pain that was her constant companion, nor the resolution that ruled her life. Markos had been her first-born. She had been unable to rear him, but no one would ever take his rightful place in her life. Marriage and a family were barred to her, she had decided. She could never hold Markos in her arms again, but no other child should supplant him in her heart!

'Karis . . .' A strong hand gripped her shoulder, the painful grasp of fingers returning her to the present as she winced beneath their pressure.

Blinking in astonishment, she realised for the first time that she had actually entered the foyer of the hotel and was half-way across the space separating the reception desk from the boutique.

'Mr Christianides . . .' Impossible to pretend she didn't recognise him.

'What's the matter?' He lifted his other hand to hold her chin, his dark eyes taking a toll of her pale face. 'Are you so distressed to see me?'

If he only knew what she'd been suffering! She made herself smile, a muscular movement of her lips which didn't fool him for a moment, if the frown which greeted it was anything to go by. 'It's colder out than I expected,' she excused herself, blinking away the tears conjured up by memory. 'And quite windy too. I think I've got make-up in my eyes.'

'They seem all right to me.' His unblinking stare dwelt on the soft turquoise behind the flickering lashes, and she was conscious again of the odd currents of unspoken feeling that surged between them. Poles apart, she thought, and this time her smile was genuine. She and Nik Christianides were like opposing poles, creating a natural if inexplicable friction when they were near one another that would always drive them apart. Even as strangers, both had been innately aware of it. 'I was hoping we could have lunch together,' he went on. 'Talk about old times?'

'I've already eaten, I'm afraid.' Karis was composed now, the rapid pulse at her throat beginning to quieten. Hadn't she already suffered, whatever harm his presence could cause her? It was absurd, this premonition of menace that affected her when she was close to him. Gaining confidence, she asked brightly, 'Are you staying here at the Acropolis?'

'Yes.' The monosyllable was terse, confirming her worst fears. 'How about dinner tonight?'

'Out of the question. To be honest, I'm not all that keen on discussing old times. Are you in London for long?'

'As long as it takes.' He tightened his grip on her arm as she tried to pull away. 'Are you usually so unsociable, or is it just me, Karis?' he asked bluntly.

'Probably a mixture of both, Mr Christianides,' she admitted coolly, determined not to betray how much his presence bothered her. 'I just can't see anything profitable coming out of our spending time together.'

'Can you not?' His smile taunted her, the dark eyes behind their thick curtain of lashes gleaming with suppressed unfriendly amusement. 'I think I'm going to prove you wrong, Miss Leeman—and have a lot of pleasure doing it!'

He released her arm, and she straightened the disturbed wool as if she were a bird grooming disarranged plumage. In truth his arrogant statement *had* ruffled her feathers, although logic told her there could be no substance to it.

'You'll forgive me—I have to get back to work.' She didn't wait for his reply, neither did she turn round as she reached the entrance to the boutique.

Richard Mansell greeted her with a smile. 'Fortune's certainly smiling on you today,' he announced. 'With a bit of luck, your sales figures are going to hit an all-time peak.'

'Tell me more!' she invited, handing her coat over to Annabel to hang up for her.

'We've got a special request lined up for five-thirty this afternoon.' He paused to shoot her a sharp glance. 'You won't mind staying overtime to do it?'

'Of course not!' She was mildly surprised he had asked her. Her time was entirely at the company's disposal—he knew that. 'What is it this time—diamond bracelets for an Arab's harem?' she queried lightheartedly.

Richard laughed. 'Not quite. Diamond and sapphire rings.'

'Mmm—lucky girl! I take it the guest's been checked out?'

This time Richard grinned. 'Couldn't come more genuine. The customer's our worthy landlord— penthouse suite. The security guard's been warned to be available to escort you there. I offered to take up the samples myself, but the customer was adamant that you should do the presentation. It seems he's insistent that he should see the rings displayed on a female hand to assess their appearance in wear.'

'No problem.' The request was not unusual. Karis drew a small pad towards herself. 'I suppose I ought to know, but I'm afraid I don't. What name does "our worthy landlord" go under?'

'As a matter of fact, I'm not surprised by your ignorance. The Acropolis Group has recently been subject to a merger. The new owners are Christianides Hotel Group, and the gentleman who has commanded your present is their executive director—Nikolaos Christianides.'

CHAPTER TWO

SEVERAL hours later Karis lectured herself sternly, albeit silently, as she replaced her make-up in the luxurious visitors' powder-room on the ground floor. There was absolutely no reason why she should feel threatened, either by Nik Christianides' presence or his ploy to get her to visit his room.

True, his being here in London had touched the scars that seared her heart with the unforgiving finger of remembrance, but that was hardly his fault, and she had long come to terms with the fact that they could never heal. As for the private jewellery showing, this was nothing new, and a service Harvey and Praxel were pleased to offer to their discerning and reliable customers, many of whom preferred to select their expensive gifts at leisure in the privacy of their own room.

She even managed to smile at her image in the mirror, recalling Nik's suggestion that a meeting between them could result in a profitable outcome. Seeing that he had already arranged a preview with Richard Mansell, his oracular statement was no longer either disturbing or astonishing! Lucky Andriana Christianides, to be the recipient of so beautiful a gift!

Returning to the foyer, Karis found the security guard already waiting for her, the tray full of expensive rings locked and discreetly placed in a briefcase unobtrusively chained to his wrist.

She wondered inconsequentially if Nik would be alone in his room. Presumably his wife wasn't with him, or there would have been no need to specify that he wanted her to accompany the rings rather than Richard.

Minutes later her assumption was proved correct, as, dressed in dark slim-fitting trousers and a casual open-necked black silk shirt, Nik himself opened the door to them, standing back with detached interest as the security man ensured that there were no undesirables lurking in the large sumptuous suite.

'In your own interests, sir,' he explained to the patiently waiting Greek, 'as well as Miss Leeman's. Take your time with your selection—I'll be waiting outside when you've finished. Miss Leeman knows the drill.'

'I'm sure she does.' Nik smiled thinly, ushering the man through the main door, before turning his attention to Karis, who was busy unfastening the coded lock of the case. 'You always dealt with problems in a most competent fashion, if I remember correctly, Karis.'

'Thank you, Mr Christianides.' She accepted his remark as a compliment, although there was nothing on his watchful face to indicate that he intended it as such. The clasps undone, she removed the velvet tray with its precious burden of gold and platinum set with fine stones. 'These are the rings you requested to see,' she said politely.

'Indeed?' He cast a quick glance at the scintillating tray. 'Shall we sit down and discuss the matter at our leisure? I see no reason why we can't do business in a civilised manner.'

He led her to where two black leather armchairs fronted a low coffee-table and indicated that she sit down. She did so, arranging her skirt primly over her knees and putting the ring tray down on the table in front of them as Nik took the chair facing her. 'Do you have any particular style in mind?' she asked brightly. 'Cluster, crossover . . .'

'I see you wear no rings yourself.' Cool, cynical eyes

fastened on her graceful pink-tipped fingers. 'Do you still prefer playing the field in preference to settling for a steady relationship?'

Karis's breath caught in her throat, a slow-growing anger unfurling inside her at his impertinence. Whatever he knew or thought he knew about her past had nothing to do with the present! But time had taught her to discipline her feelings—especially where business was concerned.

'With respect, my private life has nothing to do with you, Mr Chris . . .' she started tartly, only to have her sentence truncated.

'Your Greek accent is perfect, Karis, but you'll find it easier to call me Nik.' He sat there, sardonic eyes fixed on the tight line of her mouth.

'I was never on such familiar terms with you,' she retorted coldly, only to find he pre-empted her again before she could tell him she preferred to keep it that way.

'That must have made me the exception amongst all the young bucks in the neighbourhood.' His voice was as expressionless as his face as she stared at him in chill disbelief. If he expected some kind of apology or explanation for what had happened to her in Crete, he was going to be disenchanted.

'You sound disappointed, *Nik*,' she emphasised his name with slicing contempt, glad to hear that her voice didn't echo the shakiness of her emotions. 'But whatever my reputation was, I don't think I was labelled as a husband-snatcher.'

'No,' he agreed silkily, 'I don't believe you were. Just an English whore who had so many lovers that she was unable to name the one who fathered her child!' He watched her derisively as every vestige of colour drained from her face, and she rose unsteadily to her feet, maintaining her dignity with a visible effort.

'I thought you invited me here to choose a ring, not to

insult me.' She reached across the table to lift the velvet-lined case and found her hands gripped in an iron hold.

'You'll leave when I decide, Karis, and not one moment earlier.'

She stared up into his grim and forbidding face, her heart in her mouth.

'You seem to forget the security guard outside,' she reminded him tersely. 'All I have to do is to transmit an electronic signal and you'll find yourself with a lot of embarrassing questions to answer!'

'Press it, then,' Nik encouraged her, 'and we'll see who's most embarrassed—one of the directors of this establishment or the pretty girl who used her positon as a sales assistant to proposition him, and screamed wolf when she found he wasn't interested. It would only be your word against mine, with all the evidence on my side. I don't expect your employers know of your interesting history, do they?'

He gave a low, triumphant laugh without any kind of humour at the shocked look on her face, his eyes coldly brilliant, totally devoid of sympathy for the ordeal he was submitting her to.

'Second thoughts, Karis?' he murmured. 'How very wise. I suggest you sit down again and we can continue our reminiscences. After which we can look at the baubles you've brought with you. Who knows, I may allow you to tempt me after all.'

His promise was deliberately ambiguous as his dark eyes mocked her, and Karis's hands released their grip, acknowledging defeat. This arrogant puritan would have no compunction in blackening her name, she knew it. Even in these so-called liberated days the exclusive company of Harvey and Praxel would balk at having an unmarried mother managing one of their branches.

Yet even though a dénouement would mean her career

hopes being irretrievably demolished, the greater punishment would be the public revelation of the ever-constant pain that losing Markos had inflicted on her. Even after five years the hurt was still raw, and it took all her strength of will not to resort to alcohol or sleeping tablets to achieve the dreamless sleep that so often eluded her at night. She had come to terms with Yanís's death—but Markos . . . If Nik did but know it, *that* agony would make the darts of his scorn insignificant in comparison.

'So . . ' He leaned back contemplatively in his chair, long dark-clad legs thrust out before him, while Karis clenched her jaw, determined not to show any emotion. 'You've changed a lot since I last saw you. The teasing teenager grown into the enigmatic woman.' His head tilted sidways as he regarded her through half-closed eyes. 'And age has lent you an even greater beauty: fine bones unblurred now by youthful plumpness, skin as clear and eyes as bright as the colour of the shallow sea on sand, hair still the colour of polished tola wood . . .' The soft words flattered her, but she stayed silent, knowing intuitively that he hadn't finished. She hadn't long to wait for the *coup de grâce*. 'Tell me, Karis,' his deep rich voice exhorted her, 'what brought you to the Acropolis—the desire to entrap a rich tourist? A Greek perhaps? Did you regret the boys you had to leave behind and hope to find their adult counterparts here?'

Karis drew in a deep breath to control the wave of nausea that assailed her. Did he really expect her to treat such a loaded question seriously? All right, so she'd play it his way, she decided with a sudden spurt of spirit. 'How clever of you to guess; she said sweetly, crossing her legs seductively, and waving a high-heeled shoe nonchalantly in his direction, masking her seething fury. 'I expect you know there's a school of thought that says the Greek is the only true *macho* man left in existence—wild, passionate, determined——' She paused to analyse the effect of her statement, but apart from a hardening of his beautiful mouth Nik betrayed little reaction. Carelessly she continued, demeaning his sex and his nationality with scathing praise, 'They say, once you've had a Greek, no other man can truly satisfy you.'

'And who better than you to know?' A dark, magnetic current seemed to flow between them, a frightening force that made Karis instantly regret her words. 'Well, *agapi mou*, you've come to the right place, then, haven't you? Tell me, what's your current price?' Nik asked softly.

Dry-mouthed, Karis found herself lost for a pert reply. The hooded eyes that met her own startled gaze were unreadable as a strange heat spread its tentacles through her veins. Nik Christianides wanted her? Or was it an act to make her feel uncomfortable? It was certainly doing that, but an inner sense warned that despite his holier-than-thou stance, Nik was not immune to her as a woman even though he despised her.

What a fool she'd been to antagonise him when all the trump cards were in his hand! She'd been so sure of his innate puritanism; now she suspected it might be an assumed cloak to hide a more than usually sensual nature. At eighteen it was understandable that she'd been fooled by him, but now . . . She couldn't take her eyes from his face as every fibre of her body quivered in response to the aura of desire emanating from his lean, commanding body.

'What's the matter, Karis?' he asked gently as she rose to her feet in confusion. 'You never used to be so fussy. Six years ago you performed for the joy of it. Now I'm quite prepared to accept that there's a price to sharing your favours. Name it—I'm not a poor man!'

'This—this is ridiculous . . .' She held out her hand palm outwards as if she could prevent him from

approaching her, her original bravado swallowed by a real
fear. As a last resort she could summon the security
man—but only as a last resort!

In her own interests she must try to make Nik see he
had made a mistake about her. A bubble of hysterical
laughter rose inside her. If only he knew the truth! Far
from being a woman of unlimited experience, she had
made love to only one man—and that man just once!
Kind, loving, compassionate Yanís, whose tenderness
hadn't been sufficient to prevent his inexperience making
her first attempt at lovemaking disappointing and painful.

'I'm not promiscuous!' she flared up at her tormentor
as he held her firmly by her upper arms.

'No?' Nik pulled her against his hard body. 'What
other name is there for a girl who doesn't know the name
of her child's father?'

'I—I did know it,' she protested. 'It just wasn't
possible to reveal it.'

'Huh!' Nik made a sound of disgust. 'You expect me to
believe that?'

'I expect nothing from you!' she cried hoarsely,
determined not to give him the satisfaction of an
explanation or to sully Yanís's memory by discussing him
with Nik.

'And that's another mistake!' The next moment Nik's
hands had moved, one sliding round her shoulders,
moulding her to him, the other fastening on the back of
her head, fingers twisting through the plaited coil,
pinioning it so that his mouth could possess her own
without a fight. It all happened so quickly that she was
powerless to resist, her body bending backwards beneath
the assault. It was a savage kiss, totally selfish as Nik
despoiled the warm depths of her mouth, forcing her soft
lips to part with an invader's lack of consideration.
Taking everything, giving nothing, he left her bruised

and shaking when he finally withdrew his ravaging mouth from its victim.

Gasping to re-inflate her empty lungs, Karis raised her fingers to her head where Nik's predatory clutch had dislodged the anchoring clips of her neat hairstyle. Scarcely aware of what she was doing, she pulled out the remaining clips to free the heavy shoulder-length plait, intent on rebinding it to preserve her image before summoning the security guard.

'That's much better.' Nik's low growl of approval was her first intimation that he was watching her manoeuvre with close attention. 'Leave it loose like that. It reminds me of the very first time I saw you, lying like an innocent nymph in the afternoon sunshine, all cream and gold like a Titian beauty.' His lips curled with amusement. 'A simplistic and ironic impression, as later events proved. Come, Karis, I'm still waiting for your answer. How much do you want to spend the night with me, eh?'

'All the gold in Fort Knox wouldn't be enough!' she spat at him as with deliberate fingers she replaited her hair, ignoring his frown, imagining his incredulity if she were to tell him of her personal vow of lifelong celibacy. 'And I warn you, regardless of consequences, if you come near me once more I shall call for help.' She inhaled a deep breath, angry with herself because for a moment in Nik's arms she had experienced an incredible sense of physical awakening, and furious with *him* for the liberty he had taken with her. 'If you buy your wife a piece of jewellery every time you're unfaithful to her she must have more pieces than the Queen of England—you hypocrite!'

She made a movement towards reclaiming the jewel case, but suddenly Nik was in front of her, barring her way, his dark eyes glittering with an emotion she couldn't put a name to. Instinctively she shrank away from him. It seemed she had caught him on the raw at last by reminding him of his marital obligations. But her triumph was short lived as he rasped with violent emphasis, 'You're wrong! The only thing Andriana possesses now is the marble headstone that marks her grave.'

Karis gasped as Nik's crude statement acted like a body blow, depriving her of the breath to speak. It was the last thing she had expected. His wife was dead? But she had been only a couple of years younger than Nik himself. She had never met Andriana, but Elizabeth had described her—a beautiful girl, gentle and ethereal but with such a loving nature that she hadn't an enemy in the world . . .

For a few seconds she stared at Nik helplessly, the air between them static yet vibrant with feeling, as she smothered an impulse to throw her arms round him, to let him feel, without the need for words, the sympathy flowing from her body. She too had mourned a young life, grieved for the sheer wastefulness of it. In that instant Nik ceased to be the imperious enemy, and became just another human being who had suffered tragedy, and in that moment of shared understanding she felt only pity for him. The impulse to offer physical comfort quelled by her better judgement, the sympathy remained.

'I'm sorry, Nik,' she told him softly. 'I had no idea.'

'Why should you have?' he asked wearily. 'It was an illness—chronic liver failure. A transplant might have saved her, but there was no donor available.'

'Was it—recent?' Karis asked tentatively.

'Just over a year ago.' The fleeting emptiness she had glimpsed in his eyes vanished, to be replaced with an expression of irony. 'Time enough for my tears to dry and my mourning beard to be shaved . . . and for me to attempt to fill the gap she left in my life.' One firm, long-fingered hand rose to his face as he stroked his smooth, lean jaw as if he had in fact grown the traditional beard to signify his loss, although Karis guessed the reference had been only figurative. He cast her an assessing look. 'In the meantime I take my pleasures where I find them,' he drawled coolly.

'I dare say that's your privilege,' Karis conceded. 'You're not hurting anyone, provided your chosen partner is willing.' She was saddened by the cynical twist to his mouth. Surely she sensed an inner pain lurking within him that matched her own? It was just that he had chosen a different way of coping with it.

'Oh, I haven't sunk to rape yet, *agapi mou*, if that's what's on your mind.' His humourless smile taunted her. 'My invitation's still open, but if you choose to refuse it you're at liberty to do so.'

To her surprise he moved away from her as she shook her head, walking towards what was surely a drinks cabinet in one of the alcoves. Her assumption was proved correct as he returned bearing two brandy glasses, each half filled with a deep golden liquor.

Extending one to her, he smiled as she started back warily. 'Come, Karis. This isn't the first time you've tasted Metaxa,' he encouraged. 'And my motives are entirely pure. I don't intend to make you drunk, only to help you relax while you model some of your wares for me.'

She took the outstretched glass, surprised when he clinked his against it, murmuring *'yassou'* in the age-old Greek toast to friends. She found herself repeating the word, lifting the glass to savour the full-spirited flavour of the Greek brandy. She couldn't remember drinking alcohol so early in the evening before, but Nik was right: if she had to put up with his abrasive presence much longer she certainly needed something to relax her.

Her attention returned to the jewellery as Nik subsided once more in his chair, inviting her with a nod to start the business that had brought her to his room.

Proffering the tray in silent acceptance of his command, she watched his keen gaze rove over the glittering gold-entombed gems. 'Hmm.' He was giving the selection all his concentration, and she breathed a quiet sigh of relief that his persecution of her appeared to have stopped. 'This one—and this . . .' He lifted two rings from their velvet bed: a twelve-stone cluster and a large baguette-cut diamond with a square border of sapphires. Normal selling practice decreed that no one but the salesperson should lift the rings from their pad to guard against duplication, but Nik had forestalled her. It wasn't something she was going to make an issue of. Whatever Nik's sins, and she had no doubt they were legion, he was no thief.

Obediently she placed the cluster on her ring finger. It was slightly too large, slipping awkwardly off centre. 'Of course it could always be sized if necessary on your return to Greece,' she told him dutifully. 'Do you have any idea of the lady's preferences in jewellery?'

'I'm not even certain of the identity of the lady!' he surprised her by saying. 'There are one or two contenders I'm contemplating asking to become my wife, but they might not find the role appealing.'

That she could understand! Karis smiled spontaneously. 'So you want to persuade them with a fabulous ring? Well, this one screams of wealth!'

'Do *you* like it?' The soft question startled her and she spoke without diplomacy.

'It reminds me of a knuckle-duster.'

Nik laughed, real amusement lightening the planes of his face and taking years off his age.

'Not only do I applaud your honesty . . . I agree with you.' The dark power of his eyes lingered on her face with contemplative scrutiny. 'Which one do you like?'

It was a question she was often asked by men who wished to surprise the women in their lives and who saw some likeness between herself and the ladies of their choice. Karis had no hesitation in choosing.

'This is my favourite.' She took the gold hoop with its three parallel lines of alternate diamonds and sapphires set at an angle to the shank and slipped it on to her finger. 'What do you think?'

'Your taste is excellent. I only have to see it on your hand to appreciate its quality. I'll take it.'

He'd decided as quickly as that? Thank heavens she'd soon be on her way home. She mentioned the price to him and took a long drink of Metaxa while he produced a cheque-book. 'I take it my cheque is acceptable?' It was a rhetorical question and she answered it with a nod, looking at the thick cluster of dark hair moulding his scalp as he lowered his head to write, conscious of a strange twisting ache deep within her.

'I hope it wins you the wife you want,' she said lightly, taking her docket book from her handbag and writing his receipt, before boxing his purchase in a presentation case.

'I hope so too.' There was an odd intonation in his voice as she rose to her feet to check and lock the tray. 'I have very special requirements which most of the women of my acquaintance don't measure up to.'

'Really?' Karis slipped the combination lock on the case. 'I can imagine.' She dared to mock him now she was so nearly free of his disturbing presence. 'Let me guess—beauty, obedience, intelligence, domesticity . . .'

'Desirable—but not essential.' The atmosphere between them thickened as once more Nik's aura emitted hostility towards her. 'There is a much more important qualification I require. You see, I have a son—a boy deprived of the woman who loved him. A child who deserves better than being brought up by servants, however dutiful they may be. My only son, my heir, Karis, worth more to me than any living person now Andriana is dead.' He paused watching with what seemed a malicious pleasure the colour fade from her face. 'It's easy to find a woman to share my bed if that's what I want, but to get a good and loving mother for my son—ah, that's a very different thing. Not all women are enamoured of children—as you are well aware.'

'I hope you succeed.' She too had had a son, as Nik must know—or perhaps he had no idea what sex her baby had been. But he'd sensed her need not to discuss that episode in her past. Sensed it, and with inherent cruelty had decided to ignore it. 'I'm signalling for the security man to escort me downstairs now.' She forced herself to speak calmly, wanting only to escape from this man who was determined for some Machiavellian purpose of his own that she should acknowledge her past—as if she could ever forget it!

'Not yet you're not!' He had seen the passage of her hand towards the small electric device hidden beneath the high neckline of her dress, and aborted her action by seizing her hand in a merciless grasp. 'What kind of woman are you, Karis?' He glowered down at her with unforgiving eyes. 'It's something I've always wanted to know.'

'Let me go!' Vainly she tried to detach herself, but his other hand found her free wrist, pinioning it with steel fingers as he drew her rigid body close to his own.

'Not before you tell me what I want to know.' He was breathing heavily, glowering down at her as if he had some God-given right to demand an answer, eyes heavy with accusation condemning her without a hearing. But wait . . . Wasn't that just what he *was* offering her? Suppose she answered his impertinent questions . . . tried to justify the decision she'd made? It might not change his opinion of her, but at least it would show him that his attitude was inhuman and bigoted . . . might even make him think twice before making snap judgements on other people in future!

'Ask your questions, then!' Her chin rose arrogantly and she met his censorious gaze without flinching.

'What kind of woman bears a child and then deserts it?' he asked softly. 'That's what I want to know.'

The ache in her chest wasn't imagined, and for a fleeting second Karis wondered if her heart was actually at breaking point as she replied calmly as she could.

'A woman who puts the child's interests before her own; who has no home and no job; who knows if she takes him back to England with her that the two of them will have to live in hostel accommodation with shared kitchens and bathrooms . . .' She paused, feeling a powerful emotion building up inside her, having to fight to control the rising timbre of her voice. 'A woman who loved her baby so much she chose for him the land of his heritage where he could grow up without poverty and enjoy the birthright he deserved!'

Nik's hands were like steel hawsers round her wrists, but the pain was as nothing to the agony welling inside her.

'A woman who perhaps thought a bastard would hamper her career . . . her chances of marriage . . . a woman who was only too glad to leave her responsibility two thousand miles away and forget him?' His soft, taunting voice pierced her last semblance of control.

Possessed with uncanny strength, Karis broke Nik's hold on her and, raising her right hand, hit him as hard as she could across the cheek. It was a woman's blow, open-handed, meant to hurt but not to damage, and he bore it without wincing.

'Do you want to see me bleed?' Impossible to restrain

the tears as they welled in her eyes and trickled down her face, and the last vestige of her control snapped. She had never spoken of her feelings to anyone. No one knew of the anguish which was her everyday companion. Yanis was dead and she had mourned him. Eventually she had come to terms with her grief. But Markos—her son . . . Somewhere Markos was alive, living, breathing, learning, growing to manhood—and she wouldn't even recognise him if she saw him in the street! That was something she would never come to terms with.

'Shall I tell you that when I first came back to England I wished I could die?' She spoke through her sobs. 'That the temptation to return to Crete was overpowering, but I had no money and in any case I didn't know where Markos was, only that the family who had taken him were personally known to the doctor who arranged the adoption and he had convinced me they were kind and loving as well as financially able to give my baby everything he needed? Do you want to hear that not a day of my life passes without some part of it spent remembering my son? That sometimes I dream I'm holding him to my breast, and when I awaken the agony of loss is so great I don't get to sleep again?'

Her breath was coming in great shuddering sobs as the pent-up anguish of years poured forth as if Nik had undammed a great lake of bitterness. Words failed her, yet still she kept her luminous eyes fixed on the face of her tormentor.

Nik was standing very still, his face pale and drawn, as if he had been stunned by her angry vehemence.

'You've told me enough.' He regarded her ravaged face with dark deliberate eyes. 'Perhaps you'd like to finish your brandy now—I think you need it.'

'I've never taken refuge in alcohol.' Proudly Karis dismissed his suggestion. 'May I use your bathroom to repair my make-up?'

He indicated a door and she brushed past him, pausing only to pick up her handbag. Inside the luxuriously appointed bathroom she took her time, bathing her eyes with cold water, dusting pale blue shadow on the inflamed lids to hide their pinkness. In a few moments she would have to face the security man and the boutique's night manager. She could hardly do so in her present state.

She felt weak now, completely drained of energy. In an odd way Nik's treatment of her had engineered a catharsis, making her spill out the long-concealed bitterness at the decision she had had no option but to make and leaving her almost at peace.

He was waiting for her as she emerged.

'I could ring room service and order a meal for the two of us. Once you've seen the rings safely returned, you could come back here and dine with me.'

He actually meant it! Karis regarded his still face with horror. Was this Nik's way of apologising for the ordeal he had submitted her to?

'No, thank you.' With an effort she made her reply polite.

'We can't part like this.' He took her handbag from her, placing it on a chair before taking her gently by the shoulders. Afterwards she was never sure how it happened, but her body seemed to collapse like jelly against his strong form as he raised one hand to press her head against his shoulder, the other moving in a slow caress down her spine.

His animal warmth was comforting, the slow, sensual massaging of his hand relaxing. Off guard, she made no attempt to break free, until she felt the zip at the back of her dress slightly lowered and the cool, firm touch of Nik's fingers against the top of her shoulders, massaging them with a gentle caress.

'No! Don't touch me!' She jack-knifed away from him. It was so long, too long, some people might say, since she had been in a man's arms, and there had been something electric in Nik's soft strokes that she wasn't going to encourage. 'I've no intention of being seduced by you, Nik, so if that's what you're building up to forget it!'

'It wasn't,' he answered mildly enough. 'I have another motive in trying to persuade you to spend an evening with me. I told you my period of mourning is ended, and there's room in my house, my life, for another woman—a wife. I think the vacancy might appeal to you.'

It was unbelievable, yet Nik wasn't joking. How she knew Karis couldn't say. There was just something about him that told her he was in earnest.

'You must be deranged!' Her look was pitying. 'Quite apart from the fact that I've no intention of marrying anyone—ever—*you* would be the last person I would ever consider as a husband!' she informed him wrathfully, outraged by his complete lack of empathy. After the cavalier way in which he had treated her, he actually expected her to consider his offer? She shuddered. What motive could he have, other than making her life a living hell?

'I'm a wealthy man, Karis.' He didn't seem the least put out by her rejection. 'I have a holiday home in Crete and another on the Greek mainland, not to mention penthouse suites available to me around the world. I employ an adequate staff to see to my needs, I own three cars and a small yacht, I . . '

'That's as may be,' impatiently Karis cut in across his list of attributes. He was also an extraordinarily attractive man when he wasn't being boorish, but that too had no interest for her. 'I don't doubt that many women would be tempted by the things you can offer, but I'm not one of them. Believe me, Nik, you have nothing that would make me even consider such an outrageous idea!'

Despite her earlier protestations she suddenly felt the need for a drink. Seeing her half-full glass of Metaxa on the table, she emptied the contents in one gulp, gathered her handbag and the locked ring case with a burst of renewed energy and flipped the tiny signal that would summon the security man to the door.

'Oh, but I do, Karis!' There was no humour on Nik's dark face, neither did he attempt to approach her as she moved away from him, but his voice followed her across the room, cutting through the silence with the depth and clarity of a tenor bell. 'I have one thing I'm now convinced will make me irresistible to you. I have your son, Karis. I have Markos.'

CHAPTER THREE

THERE was a knock at the door, but Karis was in no state to answer it. Casting one searching look at her ashen face, Nik moved past her and after a cursory glance through the spy-hole in the door opened the latter to reveal the security man.

'Miss Leeman's ready to leave now,' he said smoothly.

'Right.' The guard entered, extending a hand for the ring case, a frown creasing his brow as he noticed Karis's dazed expression. 'Are you all right, miss?'

'Yes. Yes, quite all right.' Through the pounding blood in her ears Karis heard her own voice, low-pitched and trembling. 'I just feel a trifle faint.' She handed over the case, seeing as through a long dark tunnel, the guard slide it inside the chained case on his wrist. Blindly her arm reached out, seeking support. Instantly Nik supplied it, putting his strong right arm around her, pressing her firmly against his own body so that if her legs crumpled as she feared they might, there was no danger that she would fall to the floor.

'You drank that last drop of brandy a trifle too quickly, I guess.' The deep concern in his voice sounded genuine. How could he torment her like this? But she had no defence against his blithe explanation as, closing her eyes, she heard him address the other man. 'A small drink to celebrate our transaction, but it seems it wasn't a good idea on an empty stomach. Breathe deeply, Karis.' The exhortation was soft against her ear. 'Open your eyes and take one or two really deep breaths.'

She obeyed him, grateful when the feeling of nausea subsided and she could see with normal vision once more.

'Better?'

'Yes . . . thank you.' There were a hundred questions she wanted to ask Nik, but the other man was waiting patiently for her to accompany him back to the boutique. Like a hunted animal she turned appealing eyes on her predator. 'Nik?'

'Later, Karis,' he told her firmly. 'When you've returned your stock and booked in my purchase come straight back here. I'll get room service to send us up some food and we can talk about old times at our leisure.' He gave her a little push and she obeyed, like a zombie, going through the motions of a procedure she had performed many times before.

Returning to the penthouse suite fifteen minutes later, she felt as if she were dreaming, almost expecting to search the corridor for Nik's room only to find it vanished and her hopes destroyed as they had so often been in her nightmares.

He opened the door to her immediately when she knocked, standing back with a polite smile of welcome on his face. 'I'm delighted you find yourself able to accept my invitation to dinner after all,' he said suavely. 'Please make yourself at home.'

His claim to have Markos had only been a pretext to get his own way? Karis read the quiet triumph in the depth of the dark eyes that surveyed her and felt murder in her heart.

'You lied to me!'

'About Markos? No, Karis.' The dark head shook. 'Whatever reason you're here, it isn't by false pretences. Andriana and I adopted your son when you decided you could no longer look after him.'

'Oh, dear heaven!' It was a prayer, not an expletive, as

Karis sank down on the soft leather couch. 'Is he well . . .
is he happy? Oh, Nik, I had no idea . . .' She was crying
again, dabbing at her eyes with a tissue, trying to blot
their moisture. Men hated tears and she was sure Nik was
no exception.

'He's a beautiful child.' Nik's voice was gentle. 'His
health is excellent, and yes, although he missed Andriana
badly at first, children are resilient and he seems to have
regained his normal *joie de vivre.*'

'But why?' She made a helpless gesture with both
hands.

Nik stood in front of her, regarding her with thoughtful
appraisal. 'That Christmas when I saw you were
pregnant I was—concerned . . .'

'For the reputation of the hotel?' She offered him a
tearful mocking smile, not anticipating compassion.

'You were very young.' Obliquely he refused to
confirm her suspicion. 'I thought the best course for you
to take was to return to England and seek the help and
support of your family.'

'I did try, but my mother had recently remarried and
my stepfather didn't want to know.' She rested her hands
in her lap, staring down at them. The only constructive,
or rather destructive, thought her mother's new husband
had come up with was that she should have an abortion.
For some women that might have been the answer, but
not for her. She would have suffered any hardship to rear
her baby. What she hadn't been prepared to do was let
Markos share such hardship when there was an
alternative for him.

'Elizabeth implied as much when I spoke to her.' Nik
paced away, hands thrust into his trouser pockets. 'She
told me that she'd spoken to her husband about you and
he was prepared to allow you to continue in their employ
until the birth. I asked to be kept informed of what

happened. As you've already remarked, the hotel was under my aegis. I wanted no tragedies associated with it.'

He was standing with his back to her, staring out at the sky, a tall well-built man who by his claimed possession of her son wielded an absolute power over her. Karis addressed his impressive silhouette.

'I could never have managed without Elizabeth and Spyros's help,' she admitted. 'Fortunately I had a healthy pregnancy and was able to go on looking after their children right up to the birth. It was afterwards that the real problems began . . .'

It had been a difficult birth, her natural labour aborted after several hours when the baby had showed signs of distress and an emergency Caesarian section had been carried out.

'Markos wasn't born naturally.' It was a statement rather than a question as Nik gave evidence of his awareness of the facts.

'No,' she agreed, her lowered eyelashes hiding the pain that darkened colour of her eyes. 'The really fortunate thing was that I was able to benefit under some charitable trust and all my hospital bills were met. If it hadn't been for the expert attention available, Markos would have died.' She swallowed with an effort, finding it easier to address Nik's adamantine back than to watch the contempt for her which had already blazed on his face once that day. 'I was quite ill after the birth—the combined effects of a protracted labour and a major operation. I was so tired all the time and I couldn't even feed Markos . . .'

She stopped, embarrassment tingeing her parchment skin with a flush of pink. Nik wouldn't be interested in her post-natal problems. Besides, if he'd been kept informed he would know of them already. Presumably he counted them as nothing, else why should he have been so scurrilous in his scorn for the heartbreaking decision she had had to make? Homeless, jobless, ill . . . what real alternative had she had? She shrugged her shoulders, although he wouldn't see the gesture. 'That's when I made up my mind to give him a better start in life and have him adopted.'

'Andriana couldn't have children.' Nik's back was still turned to her, but the words with their husky overtones were clear and concise. 'It was the greatest regret of our marriage. When we heard of your decision we approached the hospital and offered ourselves as prospective parents. Of course, we had no reason at that time to suspect that Andriana would become mortally ill. She'd always been delicate, but then she didn't have to do any hard manual work, all that was taken care of for her. All she had to do was love the child . . .' The deep voice broke and Karis's tender heart reached out to him, but she dared not break the silence between them, waiting until Nik continued. 'Believe me, Karis, she did that with all her heart.'

'Thank you, Nik,' Karis whispered. 'Thank you for what both of you did, and thank you for telling me. I trusted the hospital. I know it was all done legally, but I always had this awful fear at the back of my mind that perhaps something had gone wrong. I couldn't have given my baby material things, but I could have given him love . . . I was just afraid it wouldn't be enough.' She swallowed resolutely, determined not to shed another tear. 'Now I know he has both, and I shall always be indebted to you.'

'I'm giving you an opportunity to repay that debt.' He turned to face her, reaching out to switch on a low-based table lamp which added a soft pink glow to the darkening room. 'I wasn't joking when I offered you marriage. Markos needs a mother.' A faint smile turned the corners of his mouth. 'All men need a mother in their formative years, to shelter them from the spartan attempts of their fathers to harden them into the male ideal. My own mother died when I was twelve, but I've never forgotten her warmth and compassion. I want that for my own son. Andriana wanted it too. Her last request was that I should replace her in my life as soon as the right woman came along.'

Karis couldn't speak. It was what he'd implied before, and she hadn't dared to believe it. Now, searching his determined face with anxious eyes, she knew he was in earnest, and felt the thunder of her heart accompany the sick excitement that curled through her.

The blue-black curly hair, coarse yet shiny with health and care, that clung to his well-shaped head and drifted across the broad forehead, breaking its clear-cut line, the deep-set, almost limpid eyes, more black than brown, the thick, dark lashes, were all proof of Nik's Greek heritage, but the elegantly long nose with its flaring nostrils, the beautiful mouth with its flowing curves, the chiselled, forceful chin claimed for him an ancestry from further East. There was something of the Arab in Nik Christianides, a frightening suggestion of seething passions she could only just begin to comprehend.

He had always possessed a dark inscrutability which, she recognised with a sudden flash of insight, had held an unwilling attraction for her on the rare occasions she had been in his company. The kind of compulsive magnetism the devil himself would exert. Karis shivered.

'You can't believe I'm the right woman for you.' She didn't want to forsake the dream he was offering her, but reality was too strong a force to deny.

'For me, no.' He was uncompromisingly honest. 'But that is unimportant. I came to London on business, having made up my mind that on my return to Crete I'd have to make a decision on remarrying for Markos's sake, then I saw you!' He took several steps forward, his gaze fixed on her face. 'It was one hell of a shock.' Dark eyes smouldered almost accusingly. 'Oh, you'd changed, but your hair and eyes and skin were unmistakable. I was never in doubt for one moment who you were. A word with the receptionist confirmed it. I also discovered you weren't married and appeared to have no stable relationship.'

'I had no idea . . .' Karis shook her head wonderingly.

'Because I made sure you wouldn't! *Panaghia mou!*' The oath was brutal on his tongue. 'Do you think I was pleased to see you? No! Yet I couldn't ignore you. I watched you, Karis, in secret—oh, for as much as a week before I approached you. As the days went by I knew I'd have to speak to you, if only to eliminate any possibility that you regretted giving your baby away.' He gave a bitter laugh. 'Andriana believed to her dying day that it was love rather than fortuity that swayed your decision, but then Andriana saw good in everyone.' Karis saw the slow passage of his larynx in the smooth column of his throat which betrayed the struggle he had won to keep his voice emotionless. 'I felt I owed it to her memory and to Markos himself to discover if there was any truth in her belief, and if so, whether you still felt the same way and were prepared to make sacrifices on his behalf.'

'Sacrifices?' Her mouth was abnormally dry.

'Tying yourself to a man without love, giving up a promising career, leaving your country.'

'I'd make them all without a second thought!' she declared fervently. A growing excitement was burgeoning inside her, stilling as she perceived the sardonic slant of his mouth. 'This isn't some kind of joke, is it? You're not lying to me, are you, Nik?' In her anguish she sprang to her feet, grasping his arms. 'You are serious?'

'Do you want me to prove the seriousness of my proposal in the traditional way?' He didn't wait for her answer, bending his head to run his soft warm lips across her own. Karis tensed, holding herself prepared for whatever might follow. 'Relax, *agapi mou*—one would never believe you were experienced in the game of love.' The hard warm lips drifted up her cheek, lingered on her closed eyelids, and then she felt his fingers on the back of her dress, and the sensation of the zip being lowered. This time she controlled the reflex flinching which would have betrayed her disquiet. Strong, gentle fingers moved slowly but purposefully, smoothing the bunched muscles at the base of her neck, sliding across the silky skin of her shoulders without further disarranging the dress.

Nik was a stranger and what he was doing was an intrusion into her privacy, but she dared not oppose him, even if his marauding touch explored further the soft secrets of her breathless body. Presumably this was one of the sacrifices he meant her to make. He didn't have to like her to take her to his bed. It would be enough that she was female and willing, and dear heaven, she *would* be willing if Markos was to be her prize! No sacrifice was too great for that, and yielding her body to the demands of her legal husband would be a very small price to pay, although he might well be disappointed at her lack of expertise.

A tiny laugh curdled in her throat at the thought. There would be many women who wouldn't see it as a sacrifice at all! Not only was Nik a beautiful specimen of adult manhood physically, but his skin had a warm, erotic scent that was exhilarating and soothing at the same time, sharpening her senses. She remembered his first angry, violating kiss, admitting reluctantly that despite the punitive power of his assault he had tasted as good as he smelled. Being Nik's wife was something she would be able to come to terms with in time . . . even in bed.

She stirred uneasily as his hands left the warm
sanctuary they had discovered to travel over the dark
surface of her dress, finding and cupping her shapely
breasts as they strained against the clinging cloth, raising
her from the lethargy she had fallen into as the painful
tightening of her newly aroused flesh sent shock tremors
through her. With slow deliberation Nik passed his thumb
across the hardened apices which were embarrassingly
obvious beneath their dour covering, his voice husky with
arousal. 'You have the body of a temptress, Karis *mou*,
but then you always did . . .'

She didn't answer, couldn't trust herself to speak, only
her eyes, wide and apprehensive, begged him for mercy.
When she saw the glint in his own eyes and the slight
smile on his mouth she knew her unspoken plea was about
to be ignored. It seemed that time was one of the things
Nik Christianides wasn't prepared to allow her. It
happened suddenly—the spasm that shot through her like
a charge of electricity, riveting her body with threads of
sensation. One moment she was holding herself rigid
trying to control the spontaneous response he was
invoking, the next it was as if she were at the mercy of
some internal earthquake—no longer in command of
what was happening to her. Yanís had been a gentle,
unpractised lover, his approach tentative and unfulfilling,
yet she had cared deeply for him. Nik was a stranger
whom she had never liked. Perhaps it was her own
heightened awareness after the day's continuing traumas,
but Nik's caresses had conjured forth a hidden spring of
arousal she had never dreamed she possessed. The
discovery was so unnerving, so unexpected that Karis
moaned, a deep exhalation of breath that ended on a sob
as her body shuddered its understanding.

Nik paused to give her one hard, fleeting look before
dropping his hands from her body and moving away from

her, his expression unreadable.

'I—don't—please, Nik . . .' Somehow he had misunderstood her reaction. Distressed by the grimness of his unsmiling jaw, aware that the prospect of her ever seeing Markos again could be hanging in jeopardy, she tried to retrieve the situation, stumbling over the words that would give her a second chance. 'What's wrong? What are you doing? I didn't mean you to stop . . .'

'It's all right, Karis,' Nik told her grimly. 'I know, in the circumstances, you would have let me make love to you if that had been my intention, but you don't have to prove anything more to me. I'm prepared to believe you really do put Markos's happiness above your own personal ambitions, and that's all I want. Agree to marry me and the contract between us won't mean you'll have to share my bed, although . . .' his dark eyes regarded her haughtily '. . . you *will* be required to accept that while *I* shall expect *you* to be celibate, the same expectations will not apply to me.'

'You—you were testing me?' Deeply humiliated, she could barely ask the question, thankful in that respect at least that he had mistaken the nature of her response.

'Something like that.' He turned his attention to her dress, fastening the zip with a careless, dismissive ease. 'Don't be alarmed. In future you'll be quite safe from my unwanted attentions provided you behave yourself. The iceberg was cooling enough for any man's ardour, but the shudder of revulsion was positively emasculating. It's a pity you didn't perfect the techniques in your early youth!'

'Nik!' Karis was horrified, frighteningly conscious that she had wounded his ego and still uncertain whether she would be made to pay for that act of *lèse-majesté*.

'Don't apologise,' he instructed curtly. 'I take it I'm right? You do want to become a mother to your son once more?'

'Yes.' Her voice cracked with emotion, and she repeated the monosyllable again to make sure he understood. 'Yes!'

'You don't need a day or so to consider the implications further?'

Did Jairus need to think twice when he had the chance of having his daughter restored from the dead? Karis shook her head. 'No.'

'Very well, then.' Nik withdrew the ring box from his pocket, pushing the lid back to extract the scintillating band of jewels. 'Give me your left hand, Karis.'

Numbly she obeyed, as he took her ring finger and fitted the sapphire and diamond band on its slender length. 'Marriage to me will give you at least two things you desire: the ring you coveted—and your son. As for the rest, who knows how many of your other dreams will stay unfulfilled? But it's a lucky man or woman who can possess everything he or she desires.' Sadness darkened his sculptured face and she knew he was remembering Andriana.

In a trice the expression was gone, to be replaced by one of arrogant command. 'For Markos's sake you and I will have to find some plane of harmony on which we can meet. It shouldn't be too difficult with goodwill on both sides, but . . .' he paused, and Karis felt her heart gather pace as he fixed her with a piercing regard, black eyes burning with a vibrant passion, 'you must always remember Markos is *my* son. When we are married he will become *our* son. He will never be exclusively *your* son. You gave up your rights to him five years ago, and whatever rights you'll enjoy in the future will be through my agency only. This arrangement between us is not for your sake, Karis, it's for my son's, and I expect you to remember that—always! Alienate him, try to turn him

against me, behave with less than the absolute propriety
your position in my household demands, and I promise
you you'll regret the day you were born!'

It was all she could do to keep her cool before the
blazing purpose that fired the darkness of his eyes. Not
trusting herself to speak, she bowed her head in a gesture
of acquiescence. Dear heaven, what sort of monster did he
think she was? If she'd needed further proof of his innate
dislike of her, this was it.

She sank down on to the couch once more as with a
brief nod, acknowledging her tacit agreement, Nik moved
to the phone, lifting the receiver and punching a number,
with a force that took no regard of its delicate electronics
but illustrated more than adequately the strength of his
feelings. 'Penthouse. We'll have the meal I ordered
served now, please.'

Replacing the handset, he settled himself down in a
facing armchair. He was matter-of-fact and coolly
detached as he began to speak, almost as if that brief
interlude of physical heat between them had never
happened. Silently Karis congratulated him, wishing her
own disturbed body would react to her mental commands
with such efficiency, but then Nik had had several days to
reach a decision. This morning, when she had got out of
bed, how could she have guessed how the day would end?
If her racing pulse and the yawning ache inside her were
anything to go by her own powers of personal persuasion
were sadly ineffective.

'I have to report personally to a board meeting in
Iraklion in two weeks' time. Since I prefer to introduce
you to Markos immediately as his new mother I think it
best we marry here in England. I believe the formalities
are quite straightforward. As far as personal papers are
concerned I shall arrange for a courier to bring mine over
to me here within the next two days. I assume a civil

wedding will suit you?' He paused, raising one eyebrow, continuing as Karis nodded, 'Invite whomsoever you wish, but I suggest you keep the numbers small and advise me in good time how many there'll be. You can give your notice in to Harvey and Praxel tomorrow, and naturally I'll pay whatever costs are incurred for breaking your contract. In fact, from this moment I'll be responsible for all your debts and future purchases. Presumably you'll want to buy a wedding outfit of some kind?'

'I suppose so.' What did you wear to marry a man who didn't love you, didn't even care for you? The job she was taking on was not really that of wife, rather that of nursemaid—but oh, to what a charge, and for the rest of her life—or at least, she amended, until Markos gained manhood. Perhaps then Nik Christianides would cast her out of his life. A terrifying thought struck her.

'Supposing Markos doesn't like me? Wouldn't it be better to let us meet first in case . . . in case . . .' She couldn't finish the sentence. What an Olympian judgement it would be if her own child rejected her!

'Of course he'll like you.' Nik dismissed her qualms with an impatient frown, spoiling what seemed on the surface to be a compliment by adding carelessly, 'He's got a naturally sunny disposition. He likes everybody. Besides . . .' impenetrable in their darkness, Nik's eyes caught and held her own, 'I'm not running the risk of reuniting the two of you unless I have legal authority over you.'

'You think I'd take Markos away from you?' Karis was shocked by his cynicism.

'Despite the seeming innocence of your beautiful blue eyes, I think you might try, despite the fact you no longer have a claim to him,' Nik confirmed bleakly.

'You really do love him, don't you?' She smiled

tremulously, thinking how ironic it was that this hard, perplexing man should feel affection for someone whose origin came from a woman he despised and a man he didn't even know.

'He's a very lovable individual—as you'll find out.'

'Would you—do you . . . that is . . .' In her anxiety Karis stumbled over her request, having to pause and take a deep breath before asking, 'Have you got a photograph of Markos with you?'

'Of course.' Nik rose to his feet, disappeared into what she assumed must be the bedroom and reappeared holding a wallet, from which he withdrew a photograph. 'Here—this is our son.'

Karis took the square of glossy paper and looked at a smiling four-year-old. Dark curly hair, perfect white teeth, a face alive with vitality and health. He could have been any well-cared-for toddler, but he wasn't. He was Markos, her baby, and before long she was going to hold him in her arms again. Hungrily she absorbed every feature on the happy face. His hair, his dark eyes, all were from his Greek father; the nose was too babyish to attribute to either of them, but surely he had her mouth? And his chin—wasn't that like her own? She lifted her hand with the expensive promise of marriage sparkling its message and ran her fingers over the softly rounded contours of her jaw, quite unaware of Nik's brooding gaze which followed every move she made.

She was glad, however, when a knock at the door heralded the arrival of dinner, and she sensed him rise leisurely to his feet to open it, because, regardless of her newly-made resolve not to irritate her imperious husband-to-be more than necessary, she had been finding it an uphill struggle to control the sudden rush of emotion that threatened to demolish her fragile self-control.

CHAPTER FOUR

NO STRANGER to restless nights, Karis managed to survive the hours of lonely darkness during which her mind bubbled with a turmoil of thoughts and suppositions, without betraying too much of her ordeal on her composed face the following morning.

In fact the cool crisp dawn found her held in a cocoon of icy calmness as she went through the familiar motions of eating a light breakfast of crispbreads smeared with low-fat spread washed down by two cups of filter coffee.

Yesterday she had been convinced Nik's proposal was genuine, and the passing hours had given her no cause to change her mind. She stared at the expensive ring on her finger. Loath to remove it in case somehow she broke the circle of fate which had drawn her back to Nik's presence, she had kept it on her hand throughout the night.

Sipping the black, fragrant brew in the porcelain breakfast mug, she welcomed the strange inertia which had enfolded her. This way she would be able to cope with the events which must take place before she achieved her heart's desire. Markos . . . Her gaze strayed to the photograph Nik had entrusted to her care. Their destined reunion was a miracle brought about by some compassionate god, and Nik was the chosen instrument of that purpose.

Despite the heat of the liquid in her mouth, Karis shivered. It was only too easy to envisage Nik as a messenger of the ancient gods: the cruel beauty of his face with its evidence of Saracen forebears, allied to the strong lithe muscularity of his six-foot-plus frame, made him a typical candidate for such a role. Yet, as in the ancient legends, there would be a price to pay for the gods' munificence. She never doubted that for one moment.

What was the easier to bear, she wondered—a life without love or a marriage without love? She'd been prepared to accept the first; now with Markos about to be returned to her, she was being offered love—maternal love—could already feel its powerful welling in her heart. Although her marriage would be a hollow one, she could and must discipline herself to play whatever part in his life Nik envisaged for her . . . and be grateful for it! What she had never sought she would scarcely miss, after all.

She finished her coffee and rose to her feet, a rueful smile curving her well-formed mouth. Meekness wasn't one of her virtues. She would hardly have achieved her present status if it had been! Hard work, study, self-discipline and a constancy of purpose linked to a flair for selling and the ability to promote her own talents had brought her from a small provincial jeweller's shop to one of the top showrooms in the country; but she could use the same qualities to transform herself into whatever it was Nik Christianides wished her to be. For the sake of what he was giving her she owed him that! Although the role had not yet been clearly defined . . .

Richard Mansell was unlocking the boutique when she arrived at the hotel, several minutes early. Following him in as he turned off the burglar alarm, Karis shrugged off her coat, hanging it neatly on a hanger in the small office, checking the lie of her white silk blouse and smoothing her straight black barathea skirt down smoothly over her shapely hips before stepping into the shop again to deliver her bombshell.

'Leaving? Marriage?' He stared at her as if she'd gone mad. 'You astound me, Karis. This must be the best-kept

secret of all time. I had no idea you were involved in that
way.' He made an expressive gesture with his hands.
'Naturally I'm pleased for you, but I hope it isn't a rash
decision you're making. Your opportunities with this
company are excellent. To throw them all up now for
marriage . . .' He paused, his raised eyebrows inviting
comment.

'I know it's sudden, Richard, but I don't need more
time.' A slight smile twisted her lips. 'Love is a very
powerful emotion, you know, and one which will
probably always influence other considerations.' He
would never guess that the love she claimed was not for
her husband-to-be . . .

She watched him shake his head, making no attempt to
disguise the scepticism of his expression. Recalling his
plump, dowdy wife with her lacklustre personality, Karis
wondered briefly if Richard Mansell had ever
experienced the strong surge of love which could lift the
human spirit to undreamed-of-heights, then immediately
chided herself for her stupidity. Looks had nothing to do
with loving, real loving. If an attractive face and figure
were all that was needed to make love bloom then she
would surely be in love with Nik, rather than regarding
him as a master whom, in her own interests, she would
have to learn to serve!

'Is there no way you can continue working after your
marriage?' His question interrupted her thought.

'Hardly.' This time the smile she turned on him was
open and generous. 'You see, the man I'm going to
marry is Nik Christianides—and I'm going back to Crete
with him.'

'Nik Christianides!' Annabel had come in unnoticed
until her shrill exclamation drew two pairs of eyes towards
her. 'Did I hear you say you're going to marry the
executive director of this hotel group?' Then as Karis

nodded, 'The man you saw yesterday? The one you told me was only an acquaintance? Oh, Karis . . . how could you! And I thought we were friends!'

Her reproachful expression brought a soft laugh to Karis's lips. 'Believe me, you're no more surprised than I am. But yesterday, when I went to his suite to show him a part of our range, he made me an offer I couldn't resist.' She held out her left hand towards the younger girl, not wishing to expand on the circumstances of Nik's proposal, and guessing the flashing ring would distract her interrogator from further questions.

'Wow!' Annabel's reaction was everything Karis had expected, as she took her hand and stared down at the diamond and sapphire band. Well versed in her trade, the younger girl needed no stock book to inform her of its value. 'That must have been some acquaintance you shared in Greece! Mind you,' she cocked her head on one side, her face breaking into a mischievous smile, 'I can understand what he sees in you. You're really quite beautiful when you relax and lose your stern expression, and your hair is gorgeous. I bet he goes crazy when you let it fall with wild abandon round your shoulders . . .'

'A bet you would certainly win if you could find anyone unromantic enough to offer you odds against it.'

At the sound of Nik's lazy voice Annabel spun round, uttering a small cry of surprise, while Karis felt her composure slipping as an unexpected blush mantled her cheeks. Unprepared for his sudden appearance, she felt her pulse quicken and cursed herself inwardly for the manifestation of colour in her face which from the humorous glint in his dark eyes had not gone unnoticed.

'I see you've told them our news, Karis *mou*.' The tiny Greek syllable at the end of her name claimed her as his possession, and she watched motionless as he approached her with a lazy grace, lowering his head slightly to rest his firm mouth on her warm cheek in formal salutation.

'Indeed she has.' Richard now accepted the inevitable with as much grace as he could muster. 'And I offer both of you my congratulations, although I shall be sorry to lose my assistant manager.'

'Ah, that—yes.' Nik smiled sympathetically at the older man. 'I've already been in touch with your head office and explained the situation. They were very understanding in the circumstances and assured me they'd be sending down a replacement later this morning.' His arm came to rest casually round Karis's taut shoulders, the fingers travelling in a slow, apparently mindless caress on the white silk of her sleeve. Today he was dressed in a silver-grey suit under which his crisp white shirt, caught at the neck by a grey and silver striped tie, clung smoothly to his broad chest. He looked self-assured and entirely in command of the situation—which was fortunate, Karis accorded ruefully, because she could feel her earlier state of mental refrigeration beginning to melt in his presence.

'This morning!' Richard was taken aback and showed it. 'But surely Karis—Miss Leeman—surely she doesn't intend to leave immediately?'

Three things happened in unison. Karis said, 'Of course not.' Nik said, 'I'm afraid so,' and the telephone rang.

'That's probably your head office on the phone now.' Nik indicated the beeping instrument with an inclination of his dark head. 'I know it must be inconvenient, but Karis and I have a lot to organise and not much time in which to do it.' The arm round her shoulder moved and she found her arm held firmly in his unrelenting grasp. 'Come along, darling,' he said calmly. 'I thought we'd have breakfast together and discuss our future.'

'I've already had breakfast . . .' Karis protested

weakly, more as a statement of fact than an act of defiance as she allowed herself to be led to the door.

'Then you can pour my coffee and watch me have mine.' Smoothly he demolished an incipient argument.

'My!' Annabel's bright eyes sparkled with admiration and something bordering on invitation as she drew Nik's attention to herself. 'Dominant with it . . .' She gave an exaggerated shiver of delight. 'I don't suppose you have a younger brother at home, do you, Nik?'

'I'm afraid not.' He met her flirtatious smile with mock-serious appraisal. 'Nor an older one, either— more's the pity.'

Annabel sighed, standing aside to let them pass, as Karis stole a curious glance at the hard profile of the man whose ring she wore. Was she imagining things, or had there been an odd inflection in Nik's reply that had hinted at a deeper meaning than Annabel's pert question had demanded?

Stepping into the waiting lift, she banished the thought temporarily from her mind. What did she know about Nik anyway? Only what she had learned through Elizabeth on the odd occasions his name had been mentioned. She could count the facts on one hand. He'd been happily married and was now a widower. He had no brothers. He was executive director of an important and extensive hotel group and he had the guardianship of her son. It wasn't an ideal basis of information for marriage, but doubtless she would learn more within the coming days.

The breakfast tray was already in place when they entered the penthouse suite. Nik seated himself at the small dining-table by the window, indicating that Karis sit opposite him as he lifted the cover from a dish to reveal a pile of warmly fragrant croissants.

'Feel free to change your mind if your appetite revives,'

he invited pleasantly, placing two croissants on a plate and helping himself to butter.

Karis shook her head with some reluctance. 'They smell delicious, but they're very fattening—especially spread with butter.'

'Really?' He feigned surprise. 'I hadn't noticed.'

Reaching for the coffeepot, Karis sighed, aware of a degree of masculine condescension in the glance that travelled over her own neat figure. With not an ounce of surplus fat on his athletic form, Nik could probably indulge himself in such high-calorie foods with impunity.

'You probably have a high metabolic rate,' she told him with a small grimace, bemoaning her own tendency to plumpness if she wasn't careful. 'How do you take your coffee—sugar and cream?' The fact that she had to ask the question showed how wide lay the gulf between them.

'Black, please.' There was humour in the dark eyes as he surprised her with his answer. 'I may have my weaknesses, but I'm no glutton.'

Conscious of his eyes dwelling on her as she dutifully filled his cup, Karis found it impossible to control the slight trembling of her hands. Perhaps she would join him in a coffee. She needed something to steady her nerves. What had Richard Mansell said? Something about not having made a rash decision. She was about to do more than that. She was about to make a rash contract with a man who was not only a stranger to her, but one whose opinion of her was abysmally low. Should she tell him the truth about Markos's parentage now, while this amicable air existed between them?

Somehow she lacked the impulse to do so. What difference would it make anyway—there was no guarantee that Nik would believe her. One look at his aggressive jawline and anyone could tell that the prepossessing man sitting opposite her was one who would believe what he wanted to, and it seemed from his previous attitude that he was already convinced she was inherently promiscuous.

'Thank you.' He lifted the cup to his lips, savouring the aromatic scent of its contents before taking a small sip. 'Tell me, Karis, is your appearance of paramount importance to you?'

'I'm not sure what you mean by paramount . . .' Startled by his question, she sought a further clue to his meaning, but could gain nothing from the blankness of the dark gaze that fastened on her own eyes. Was he accusing her of vanity now? 'It's very important for work,' she temporised. 'The more attractive the salesperson, the better the relationship between seller and buyer, especially when the product is expensive and beautiful. Good grooming is vital . . .' She glanced down at her own beautifully manicured hands. 'Who would want to buy a diamond ring from an assistant whose hands were grubby or whose nails were chipped or broken? But I'm not fanatical about it, if that's what you're asking. I like to think I could fit into any environment.' There was an element of defiance in the straight look she gave him.

'Whatever your methods for success, they appear to have worked very well.' Nik leaned back in his chair, one lean-fingered hand neatly dissecting the remaining croissant on his plate. 'What exactly did you do when you arrived back in England?'

'I went—home.' The word stuck in her throat. 'That is, I went to the house where my mother was living with my stepfather. They were the terms they'd laid down. If I came back to England without . . . without my baby there would be a room for me.' She stared down at her hands clasped in her lap. 'Having made arrangements for Markos, it seemed the sensible thing to do.' She had been

hurt by her mother's cold dismissal of her problem, but
she had felt guilty too. In Rosemary Leeman's eyes her
daughter had betrayed her upbringing. Whatever the
attitude of the media towards illegitimacy, in her
mother's eyes she had been selfish and stupid. Karis had
had to fight down the suspicion that Rosemary couldn't
have cared less about the number of men she had slept
with provided she had taken precautions against
embarrassing the older woman with a bastard
grandchild—and a Greek one at that! So she had returned
to make her peace—or try to.

'Is your natural father dead?' Nik asked into the
silence.

'Not that I know of.' Karis shook her head. 'They were
divorced when I was four—Mother discovered that he'd
got a girlfriend. After the divorce he married her and
disappeared. We never heard from him again. I . . .' She
stopped abruptly. Nik wouldn't want to hear about her
childish imaginings.

'You—what?' He was regarding her with every sign of
interest. 'You have some idea where he might be?'

'No.' Karis shook her head. 'Mother was very bitter
about everything. It's just that I used to wonder if he ever
tried to keep in touch with me and she refused to allow it.'
She shrugged her shoulders philosophically, forcing a
smile on to her lips. 'It's something I'll never know.'

'So you returned to this house where you never felt
welcome—and then what?'

'I couldn't let them keep me. I had to get a job—any
job, and fast. It was a small town and opportunities were
few, especially for girls who couldn't type and whose only
qualification was a knowledge of foreign languages. Shop
work seemed the only opening, and I was lucky enough to
get employment in a small local branch of a multiple
jewellers. I was very fortunate—staff training was

excellent and transfer between branches easy to accomplish.

'After a year I was able to leave home and work in a much larger branch in Essex.' Again she paused, afraid of boring Nik, but he encouraged her recital with a sharp nod of his sable head.

'I continued with the management training and got an award as the best trainee of the year.' She couldn't disguise the pride in her voice. The home study hadn't been easy, sharing, as she was, a tiny apartment with two other girls, but she'd persevered with all the varied facets of the trade, amazed that she could have ever thought managing a successful shop was easy!

Fascinated by the beautiful objects she handled every day, she had gone more deeply into the subject than had been expected of her, tracing the origins of the gemstones and precious metals, their long, colourful history and that of the craftsmen past and present who created such items of beauty. It had been a diversion which had paid dividends in the personal interviews given at the end of the course. In retrospect she realised that her devotion to her technical books had acted as a therapy for the loss she was bearing.

'Congratulations. Your industry impresses me.'

Uncertain whether he was being sarcastic or not, Karis lifted her chin a little higher. 'Yes—well, I *was* industrious. I had my sights set on London and the award got me an interview with Harvey and Praxel.' She had gone to that meeting with her heart in her mouth and had been chosen from a list of five candidates.

'And that was——?' queried Nik, then, seeing her look of puzzlement, 'How long ago?'

'Oh,' she pondered for a moment, 'last September. Then, when this hotel opened and they were offered the franchise of the boutique, I was asked to come here as assistant manager. I guess my knowledge of other languages influenced them,' she added as an afterthought.

'It was probably one of their considerations,' Nik agreed equably, surveying her thoughtfully. 'It seems that my proposition has wrecked your future plans completely. Let's hope you'll find the financial compensation I can offer you sufficient recompense for the loss of such splendid prospects.'

'I'm not interested in your riches, Nik.' Stung by what she saw as a cruel cynicism, Karis's eyes flashed a turquoise flame across the table. 'As manager of my own branch, which was a definite probability, I would have been on a percentage of branch turnover. I might not have aspired to your heights, but yes, I would have been amply rewarded! The fact remains that I'll gladly give it all up to be with Markos again!'

'A change of heart, Karis?' he demanded cruelly. 'An easy assertion to make when you know there's no possibility of your facing poverty again. But how will you cope with the loss of job satisfaction? I assume it was that as much as the financial rewards that drove you further up the ladder?'

There was pure antagonism in the way his eyes clashed with hers, an undercurrent of censure in the deep voice. Was he having second thoughts? Karis felt the blood drain from her face. Was this some kind of divine punishment he was delivering to her? Making her lose her job, promising her joys he had no intention of delivering? Was he about to humiliate her by calling the whole thing off?

'Well?' he prompted harshly. 'Are you sure that looking after a child will fulfil you—completely?'

Gazing into his hard-boned face, the remorselessness of his fixed appraisal, Karis felt her heart grow heavy. How could she explain to this disdainful Greek that her ambition had stemmed from the need to get away from a home where she was tolerated rather than loved, from a parent whose attentions had always been adequate but perfunctory?

It had taken her some time as a child to realise that she was too much like her father to retain a hold on her mother's heart. When Steven Leeman had left his wife for another woman he had left his daughter in the care of a woman whose bitterness at his desertion had warped her feelings for his child. She had learned, painfully, that whatever service she performed for her mother, it would never be accepted as satisfactory.

When Rosemary had remarried, Karis had thanked God she had been old enough to leave home. She had seen Elizabeth's advertisement in a magazine and had been thrilled to find herself accepted. To the lonely teenager she had been then, Crete had seemed like Paradise after Limbo. How deeply she had appreciated the warm friendliness of her employers and the spontaneous affection that had grown up between herself and Yanis and his friends. How cold, in comparison, had seemed the ambience of her mother's smart suburban detached house . . .

'You seem uncertain?' Nik's dour assertion broke into her agonised memories, drawing her sharply back to the present as he continued inexorably, 'I intend that Markos shall have first call on your time, so it's something you'd better be prepared for! Or do you want to change your mind?' Across the table he glared at her, his dark brows drawing closer across the bridge of his arrogant nose as he drew them together. 'Because if not, in ten days' time we shall be man and wife and your options reduced to nil!'

Her throat parched with nerves, Karis found herself unable to swallow. The merciless invaders who had come

from Arabia to spread their doctrines through the Eastern
Mediterranean could hardly have looked more fierce than
Nik Christianides at that moment, and she felt a shiver of
pure fear trickle down her spine. Somehow she managed
to find enough dampness on her tongue to moisten her
lips and give him the answer that his angry silence
demanded.

'The only fulfilment I want is to hold my baby in my
arms again!'

'Good!' She saw the tense lines of his face relax. 'Only,
of course, you'll find he's no baby now. At the end of this
summer he starts school. Then, more than ever, he will
need a warm, loving home to cushion him against the
rubs of growing up.' A shadow passed across his eyes as if
he was recalling his own youth and regretting it. Too
uncertain of his temper to question it, Karis sat in silence,
as abruptly Nik rose to his feet.

When he spoke again he was coolly impersonal.

'I assume you've told your landlady that you'll be
leaving, and I need to know what possessions, if any, you
want to bring to Crete with you. They'll have to be
shipped, and the sooner I can get the matter put in hand
the better. As far as your personal wardrobe is concerned,
bring everything you need and we'll pay excess baggage.'
He cast an appraising eye over her neat appearance. 'I
suggest you replenish your stock in London before we
leave. Later this year we'll return to Athens, but in the
meantime you'll probably find more to your liking here
than in Iraklion.'

'I don't think I need anything,' she demurred, realising
for the first time that she didn't even know her exact
destination. 'Where exactly shall we be living?'

'After our *meenas tou melitos* in Iraklion,' his mouth
twisted cynically as he translated the word 'honeymoon'
into his own language, 'after *that* we'll be joining Markos

and my housekeeper Maria at my villa on the south coast near Ierapetra for the summer months. I'll be able to arrange a few weeks away from business on such an important occasion, so you won't be too lonely while you're settling in.'

Lonely or unsupervised? Karis thought a little bitterly, convinced that Nik wouldn't trust her out of his sight with her own son until he'd satisfied himself that her presence wouldn't endanger the child in any way. Dear heaven, did he intend to keep her a prisoner until she'd proved herself—and exactly how would she accomplish that? She made an effort to mask her feelings, contenting herself with nodding her head in tacit agreement.

'I'm afraid I have a meeting with a bank in half an hour, so we'll have to curtail this pleasant discussion.' Nik glanced down at the thin gold watch on his sinewy wrist. 'Please feel free to use this suite as your own in my absence—the manager knows of your presence here. Perhaps you might like to spend the time informing your friends and relations of our forthcoming nuptials. I'm sorry I can't give you a precise place or date yet, but my staff are working on it.'

'Do I have any say in it?' A spurt of her old spirit made Karis ask the question as Nik made for the door.

'Of course.' He gave her a blank look, as if surprised she would want to concern herself with something so unimportant as her own wedding. 'Any ideas, let me know, and if they're feasible and legal I'll see what can be done. Oh, and while I think of it, while you're choosing your wedding outfit you'd better get yourself a formal evening dress, something seductive but not flashy.'

'But I thought evening life in Greece was very informal,' she protested, wondering who she was supposed to be seductive for. Not Nik. He had already made that abundantly clear.

'So it is—normally.' He smiled, but the amusement didn't reach his eyes. 'However, my father, who is chairman and one of the chief stockholders of the Christianides Group, will be celebrating his name day on the first day of the board meeting in Iraklion. You can be assured that the party thrown that night will be something of a social occasion.' He paused and drew one lean palm thoughtfully down his smooth jaw. 'It seems to me to be the ideal opportunity to introduce him to his new daughter-in-law, and I should like to see him impressed.'

'Impressed? With me?' Karis looked uncertain. 'I'm afraid I'm no beauty queen.'

'No, you're not.' His quick agreement was hardly flattering, but then she had been speaking truthfully, not looking for compliments. 'You have a quality about you that is much more striking than some long-legged adolescent with peroxide hair and silicone breasts.' His eyes drifted over her from crown to toe and returned to hold her gaze. 'Your little friend downstairs had something when she remarked about your hair tumbling down to your shoulders . . . You'd better find yourself a good hairdresser and get rid of that ugly construction that's about as attractive as last year's hot cross bun.'

Flushing with anger, Karis began to protest. 'It's neat and suitable . . .'

'For the job you were doing this morning, no doubt,' Nik intercepted briskly. 'Although if you hoped to detract from your obvious sex appeal it could be classed as a failure. But that job is ended now, and your new employer requires a different projection.' Dark eyes gleamed with amused understanding, as he perceived the sulky twist of her pretty lips at his didacticism. 'Come now, Karis, I'm not asking you to have a tonsure—merely to adopt again a style that you once wore so effectively. Is that so difficult?'

Damn him for this overt exercise in domination! Was she supposed to become a Galatea to his Pygmalion? The sheer arrogance of his instruction plus the condescending glint in his deep-set eyes infuriated her. What would he do if she refused? Surely not call off their wedding on such a minor point? On the other hand, she wouldn't put it past him to attain his own desires by force, and if anyone's scissors were to lop off her hair, far better it was a professional hairdresser than an irate fiancé!

'I thought you were ordering me—not asking me,' she returned sweetly, determined not to appear too compliant. 'Of course, if it's just a request, I promise to consider it.' She matched and held his gaze, seeing with an inner triumph a glimpse of something that could have been respect darken his pupils.

'It was a request, naturally.' He paused just long enough to let her taste the fruits of victory before adding, 'However, within my own sphere of influence you'll soon discover that a request from me is automatically treated as a command by those receiving it.'

'How interesting.' She was fighting him with words, aware of a tingling tension, rather like static electricity hovering between them. He was threatening her, and both of them knew it, though only Nik himself knew what penalties her defiance might bring down on her. There was too much at stake for her to oppose him as she would have loved to have done, and he was watching and enjoying her fight to control her feelings, knowing at that moment he had the upper hand.

She could only hope that in the due course of time he would get tired of baiting her and leave her alone to perform whatever domestic duties he thought proper for his wife. For the time being, at least, discretion would be the better part of valour. She took a deep breath to stop her voice from shaking with annoyance, dipping her eyelashes in mock surrender to his will.

'I'm afraid it's going to take me some time to understand what you expect from me, Nik. I hope you'll be patient while I learn.'

Beneath her lowered lashes she saw his mouth thin and knew he wasn't fooled by her fake submission, but there was no hint of laughter in his deep voice, only an overriding aura of command as he said quietly, 'Oh, you'll find I'm infinitely patient when I want to get my own way, Karis *mou*.'

The endearment again, soft and mocking, driving the irritation from her soul and leaving her feeling destitute and unhappy. Valiantly she fought the wave of misery that swept over her, holding her head high as she asked, 'Is there anything else I need to know before you go?'

'Only that I've instructed the manager to make available to you whatever cash you require for your purchases. Alternatively, I can arrange for a transfer of funds from my London account into your bank, only that will take longer.'

'Thank you. I'm well able to buy what I need from my own savings.' Proudly Karis refused his help. She had been saving hard to put down a deposit on her own house. With the favourable mortgage terms available through Harvey and Praxel to their employees, it wouldn't have been long before she owned her own property. Now the suburban house with a small garden was a lost dream, the savings available for extravagance. She would give Nik what he wanted—but it would be at her own expense, not his. That way she could retain some modicum of her dignity.

'If that's what you prefer.' He accepted her decision calmly. 'And just one thing more. If you go out, please leave a note as to where you've gone and how long you intend to be. My own movements are uncertain, but I hope we can continue our interrupted conversation over dinner this evening.'

'Why not?' Karis shrugged resignedly.

On the threshold Nik paused.

'Be careful, Karis *mou*. I wouldn't want to lose you so soon after finding you again.'

She watched the door close gently behind him before subsiding in one of the deep armchairs. What was she getting herself into? Nik was tough, hard and obviously successful. His nature was forceful and tortuous, a curious mixture of asceticism and passion . . . and a complete enigma to her. Added to which, she admitted reluctantly, he was incredibly good to look at. A fact which should have no bearing on her opinion of him, but which intruded into every judgement she attempted to make.

CHAPTER FIVE

LUNCH was served on the flight between Heathrow and Athens. With the hectic events of the past few days behind her and Nik's engraved gold ring glistening on her finger, Karis found it easy to relax in the comfortable business-class seat and enjoy the food and accompanying wine.

With formal courtesy Nik had offered her the window seat and she had accepted with pleased alacrity, anxious to experience once more the thrill of leaving the clouds of Northern Europe behind to witness the magnificent sight of the Greek Islands strung across a matchless blue sea. As a raw seventeen-year-old she had let fall a few tears of absolute joy at her first sighting of the fabulous Isles of Greece; leaving them, she had wept for another reason. Today she wouldn't embarrass the man beside her with a display of emotion, but she would feel it—increased a hundredfold at the prospect ahead of her.

The clouds were still thick beneath the airbus, only the pale blue emptiness of the stratosphere above them promising the unclouded skies yet to come, as she dealt neatly with her roast chicken and allowed her thoughts to wander back to the ceremony that was about to change her life.

Her wedding to Nik had been the first one of the morning, the pleasant registrar's office freshly polished and gently scented from the bowls of carefully arranged flowers. The ceremony had been simple and unemotional, witnessed only by two of the registrar's staff. Unconsciously Karis's mouth tightened as she

72

recalled the way her mother had received the news of her impending marriage.

Phoning Rosemary Leeman that first day in Nik's hotel room, she had waited until they had exchanged the formal pleasantries such calls customarily engendered before announcing her decision.

'Mother, there's something I have to tell you . . . I'm going to be married next week. I hope you'll be happy for me.'

The silence had been total for several seconds before Rosemary had asked casually, 'Your—er—husband-to-be . . . does he know about—what happened to you in Crete?'

'Markos?' Karis had given an odd little laugh at her mother's predictable reaction. 'Oh, yes, Nik knows all about Markos. In fact it was Nik who adopted him.'

'I see.' Rosemary's flat tone contradicted the intelligence she claimed. 'You're going to marry a Greek, then?'

She'd made it sound as if the Greeks were one step removed from Martians but Karis had persevered, something inside her driving her to find some platform of understanding with the woman who had borne her.

'Yes, he's Greek. I knew him vaguely when I was over there, and recently we met again in London.' She had waited for the further questions a concerned mother might ask—what was his name, what did he look like, what job did he have . . . When none was forthcoming she had broken the empty silence herself, her fingers gripping the receiver so tightly that the knuckles turned white. 'Oh, Mother, don't you see what it means? I get my son back again! My son—your grandson . . .' Her voice had tailed away as she had controlled the break in her voice before adding, 'Nik and I would like you to come to our wedding. It'll be in a register office, of course . . .'

'Of course.' Rosemary's voice had been coolly patronising. 'Well, I hope you know what you're doing. Next week, did you say?' She had paused as Karis had waited, guessing it was only an imaginary diary which was being thumbed through. 'I'm afraid Harry and I are going up to Scotland next week for a few days—a sales conference—but of course we'll be thinking of you.'

A few trivial comments later and both receivers had been replaced. Three days afterwards Karis had received a cheque for two hundred pounds drawn on a joint bank account. Nik, to whom she had confided the result of her brief phone call, had taken the slip of paper from her hands, regarding it thoughtfully for a few seconds, then tearing it in half and dropping it into the waste-paper basket, before turning to capture her wide-eyed gaze with an insolent stare.

'You wished to cash it? Buy yourself something to remember them by, hmm?'

'No,' she had replied firmly, earning herself a brief nod of approval. 'No, I want nothing from them.' Only the things they'd never been able to give her—love and understanding and their blessing, she'd added silently to herself. The things that life had destined she should never have.

Despite the early hour of her nuptials, arranged for the convenience of boarding the mid-morning flight from Heathrow, and the lack of guests, Karis had refused to be daunted. Nik had expected she would buy herself a special outfit for the wedding, and that was just what she had done.

Some girls might have dreamed of a white wedding, of lace and tulle, buttonholes and bouquets, but that had never been Karis's ambition. Neither had she felt a church service to be more binding than the legal agreement she was about to make. Surely the important thing was how sincere one was in one's heart—not the outward show of pomp and circumstance? She would dress as if it were for a special occasion—as indeed it was! There might be no love between herself and the striking Greek whose first allegiance was to his adopted child, but neither was facing the undertaking of marriage lightly!

When she had set eyes on Nik as he'd broken with tradition to collect her from her flat that morning she had been glad she'd taken such pains with her appearance. Magnificently groomed and dressed in a pale fawn suit, a brown and gold silk tie at the neck of a champagne-coloured shirt, her bridegroom was every inch the ardent suitor in appearance—from the immaculately polished shoes to the scarlet carnation in his buttonhole.

His slow, appreciative gaze had travelled over her, dark eyes approving her newly trimmed and layered hair, its soft tendrils curling disarmingly from the half-fringe which feathered across her forehead to the shoulders of the fitted mint green linen suit she had purchased in New Bond Street. With its low U-shaped neckline, padded shoulders, six-buttoned front and waistcoat-pointed jacket over the newest, slim-fitting, short-length skirt, the suit had exercised a powerful appeal to her.

Dismissing the thought that, since it was undoubtedly too smart for Iraklion and Nik was hardly likely to seek her company as a travelling companion to more fashionable cities, she would probably never wear it again, Karis had chosen her accessories with care to contrast sharply with its pale purity: scarlet leather gloves, toning red suede Louis-heel shoes with bows on the instep and a matching suede handbag. Adorning the pale skin round her neck she had worn a simple gold leaf curled to hold one tiny perfect pearl, the whole creation suspended on a fine gold chain. She had bought it for herself to celebrate her latest promotion, never dreaming at the time of the first occasion on which she would wear it . . .

A movement beside her drew her attention to Nik as he lifted her empty tray from the table in front of her and handed it to the waiting stewardess. How quiet he'd been since the ceremony, locked in his own thoughts, excluding her from whatever problems or pleasures lay ahead. A sense of loneliness flooded through her. She had known what to expect, but it would take some getting used to! Dared she hope that when they knew each other better Nik would deign to converse with her, share something of his busy life?

Opening her bag to locate the means of refreshing her make-up, she was assailed by the sweet fragrance of freesias, her heart twisting painfully as she aught sight of the delicate rose, lemon and purple blooms. She had been touched and thrilled when Nik had produced the small spray and fastened it to her jacket, before leaving her flat for the last time. Loath to abandon it at the airport as he had suggested, she had insisted on taking it with her, concealed inside her bag. Lifting the blossoms to her face, she inhaled their gentle perfume. The buttonhole had been well wrapped and sealed: a drink of water on arrival and it would last several days yet!

Aware of the sidelong, half-amused look of the man at her side, she decided to ignore it. Probably Nik thought she was being absurdly sentimental about something which was merely traditional, but a bride was allowed some fantasy on her wedding day, wasn't she? If she wanted to pretend the thoughtful gesture had been occasioned by some tiny element of caring then she wouldn't allow his scorn to crush her dream! Replacing the spray, she found her compact, glad when Nik returned his eyes without comment to the magazine he'd been reading.

After a brief wait at Athens to change planes they

landed in Iraklion shortly before eight in the evening, local time, clearing Customs with a minimum of delay and finding no difficulty in obtaining a taxi for the short ride to the centre of the town.

The evening air was cool as Karis alighted from the cab outside the familiar entrance of the Christianides' oldest hotel on the island. Entering the foyer, she was surprised to find it smaller than she had anticipated, housing only the reception desk, padded bench seating and four lifts.

'The lounges and bars are all on the first floor,' Nik explained patiently, seeing her look of surprise. 'The rest of the ground floor is let out to shops, but I don't think you'll be disappointed with the décor, or the suite that's been reserved for us.'

'Congratulations, Kyrios Christianides!' The bellboy's dark eyes dwelt fractionally but admiringly on Karis as he lifted their suitcases and preceded them into one of the lifts. 'Everyone here is delighted with your news. We wish you and your lady every happiness.'

'Thank you.' Nik's grave reply gave nothing away as he waited patiently for the lift to stop on the twelfth floor and the boy to open the door to the penthouse suite.

'Oh, it's beautiful, Nik!' The small and rather sombre entrance lobby hadn't prepared Karis for the size or opulence of the room—oatmeal-coloured carpeting, rose and oatmeal curtains, a circular teak and glass table surrounded by half a dozen chairs, three soft pale coffee leather armchairs, television, subdued, concealed lighting on the walls and two beautifully designed glass table lamps at strategic locations were among her first impressions.

'I'm glad you like it,' Nik smiled with quiet satisfaction. 'I think you'll find the bedrooms equally attractive.' He led her through an archway to a small lobby, opening one door after another as he spoke. 'This

is the main bedroom . . . this is the second one . . . and
here is the bathroom.' He paused momentarily as she
nodded her approval of everything she had seen. 'Do you
have a preference as to which bedroom you have?'

A wave of relief flooded through her. So Nik *was* going
to honour his promise not to share her bed! For the first
time Karis admitted to herself she had been subject to a
growing anxiety about the reliability of his earlier
undertaking. Not that she was irresistible—but Nik,
despite the self-control she had seen evinced at their first
meeting, was all man and she was now his legal wife, and
therefore, by the standards of his culture, automatically
available.

Of course mentally he despised her, she was in no
doubt of that, but men were not renowned for being too
concerned with conscience when their virile bodies
clamoured for release, and she was uneasily aware that,
despite his better judgement, Nik was not beyond being
aroused by her presence even though that arousal was
based on desire, not affection. No one knew better than
her husband, either, that in her present position she was
in his absolute power.

Markos was his to share or to conceal according to his
whim, and there was virtually nothing she wouldn't be
prepared to do to see her son once more. Sharing a bed
with Nik would have been a disturbing ordeal, even
sharing a room would have fed her apprehension, but this
arrangement was ideal.

Flashing him a smile compounded of relief and a real
appreciation of the luxury of her surroundings, she said
lightly, choosing the slightly smaller accommodation, 'I'll
have the blue room, if that suits you.'

'For the time being it does.' His long, slow look
encompassed her from head to foot before he turned to
collect her case, lifting it easily on to the rack inside her

chosen room. 'As you see, you have your own TV and a selection of books to amuse you if you want an early night.' He walked to the window, pulling the curtain aside to stare out into the darkness. 'When morning comes you'll find you also have a very pleasant balcony overlooking a small garden.'

'It sounds ideal.' Karis kept her voice light. It also sounded as if she was being confined to lonely seclusion! 'How long are we spending here?'

'Two or three days . . .' Nik shrugged a nonchalant shoulder. 'Two days of conference, and then it'll depend on what other business there is for me to do.'

'I see.' Suddenly tired, Karis moved forward to sit on the bed, swinging her legs up thankfully beneath her. 'While you're working I'd like to reacquaint myself with Iraklion—take another look at the museum, things like that, if you've no objections.'

There was a slight edge to her tone and the quick lift of Nik's eyebrows showed her it had been perceived, but he was unruffled as he replied easily, 'Of course you must amuse yourself as you think fit in my absence. I'm afraid I won't be available to spend much time with you during the day, but since you're no stranger to the city I fancy you won't find that too much of a loss.'

Dark eyes challenged her as a ripple of tension spread between them and Karis felt a qualm of unease thrill through her. Did Nik want her to confirm or deny his assumption? Intuition told her that either course promised her conflict as his tall figure loomed over her. A feeling of despair brought a sigh to her lips. How could she even start a satisfactory relationship with this difficult Greek unless he gave her some clue as to what he expected from her?

'You're tired.' His flat tone unexpectedly released her from her quandary. 'I suggest you unpack what's necessary, freshen yourself up and I'll see you outside in the lounge when you're ready for a pre-dinner drink.' On the threshold he paused, turning to rest his gaze on her pale face.

'Which would you prefer—to dine here or go down to the dining-room?'

If they had been on the kind of honeymoon girls dreamed of there would have been only one answer, but what pleasure could there be in sharing an intimate meal with the taciturn man she had married?

'I'd like to see the dining-room,' she decided, phrasing her answer as tactfully as possible. 'If the public rooms are as splendid as the private ones it should be very attractive.'

'I think it is,' he told her curtly. 'So be it, then.' The door closed quietly behind him as Karis flung herself backwards, burying her head in the soft pillow. The first few days were bound to be awkward, but with the thought of seeing Markos a gleaming goal for her, she must do everything in her power not to alienate Nik.

It was nearly two hours later that, refreshed and unpacked, she went into the lounge, having changed her suit for a high-necked, long-sleeved floral dress of Chinese silk, its beautifully cut bodice and slim-line skirt eminently flattering to her curvaceous slenderness, the predominant colours of gold, turquoise and scarlet an eye-catching mixture. Nik's deep tones came clearly to her as he spoke softly on the telephone. Hearing her arrival, he turned his head briefly towards her, then flicked a switch on the instrument. Immediately from the built-in loudspeaker Karis heard a child's voice speaking excitedly.

'. . . And I saw a big swan all made out of butter and a 'normous fish all covered in pink stuff, and Tonia told me it was mashed potato, but Daddy, it was pink! So I knew she was teasing me . . .'

Transformed by his smile, Nik's face lost its Saracen severity as Karis gasped her shock and reached to support herself against the wall. It was her son speaking.

'It sounds like you and Tonia had a great time, but the party was for my guests at the Supermare. I hope you left them something to eat.'

''Course I did!' The childish voice was scornful. 'There was lots and lots, whole tables full. Tonia and I just had a little bit of the *calamari*. When are you coming home, Daddy?'

'As soon as I can, Markos *mou*, two, maybe three days, and I'm bringing someone with me who wants very much to meet you.'

A cold hand clutched at Karis's heart. Suppose the child's innocent voice should declare that he couldn't care less about his father's 'friend'? The pulsing blood of fear was pounding so rapidly against her eardrums that she nearly missed Markos's retort.

'Will he take me on the beach when Tonia's too busy, and take me to see Kostas's new kittens?'

Nik's throaty laugh echoed round the room. 'We'll all go on the beach and to see Kostas's kittens—but Markos, listen, this special person who wants to meet you is a *lady*, and something else—I bet she knows just how to make pink mashed potatoes!'

The clear sound of a child's giggle came from the speaker, followed by a silence and then the question, 'Is this lady like Nikoletta, Daddy?'

'Nikoletta?' There was no disguising the surprise that coloured Nik's ejaculation, before he answered, 'No, *yiós mou*, she is like no one but herself.

'I thought you'd like to hear his voice.' Calmly he replaced the receiver after bidding the child goodbye and exhorting him to have sweet dreams. 'Although it seemed a little premature to invite you to speak.'

'I wouldn't have known what to say,' Karis agreed sadly, choosing an armchair and sinking into its depths. 'There's so much I need to know before we meet.' Her troubled eyes darkened as the pupils dilated. 'Does Markos know he's adopted—does he know that Andriana is . . .' Her courage faltered as her mouth refused to utter the cruel word.

'Dead?' Nik's tone was bitter as he walked towards a large built-in refrigerated cupboard at the far side of the room. 'Yes, Markos knows about the finality of death, and he knows too that Andriana became a mother to him only when his natural mother rejected him . . .'

'I didn't reject him! I loved him!' Karis was on her feet, eyes blazing. Nik was hurting and determined to share his pain with her, but the unjustness of his accusation was a wound she wouldn't accept. She was across the room, seizing his arms, digging her fingers into the hard flesh beneath the elegantly tailored sleeves, her voice harsh with passion. 'I may be guilty of many sins, but rejecting Markos isn't one of them. I gave him up, yes! But that's not rejection. I loved Markos! I tell you, I loved him, and if you dare to accuse me of that again I'll . . .'

'Yes, *agapi mou* . . .?' The soft query from the harshly twisted mouth was almost obscene. 'What will you do?'

How could she answer? *Wipe that sardonic smirk off your face . . . tear you limb from limb . . . pound you with punches until you're senseless?* Even if physical violence hadn't been anathema to her, she was incapable of using it against Nik's superior strength, and verbal violence would only demean her.

'Never forgive me?' Nik answered the question for her, his expressionless gaze absorbing her hostile eyes, her trembling mouth, her heaving chest as she fought to control her anger. 'Then here is something else to add to my crimes.'

Before she could move he had imprisoned her, one arm binding her to him as the other hand laced through the wealth of hair curling against her head, drawing her face towards his own, her lips towards his mouth as inexorably as thunder follows lightning. Karis fought his kisses, her heart churning, her blood at fever pitch, recognising it for what it was—the stamp of absolute possession.

Long afterwards in the quiet darkness of her own bedroom she was to admit that Nik's assault had been determined but not brutal. At the time she had only known that she lacked the strength and purpose to repel his rapacious mouth and marauding tongue, that they had conquered her not as a demonstration of love but as proof of mastery.

'Do you prefer wine or brandy?' Nik's cool tone shamed her agitation as, releasing her, he opened the cabinet displaying a selection of glasses.

'Wine, please.' Following his lead, Karis swallowed her helpless fury. Brandy would sound as if she needed a restorative. She did! But she was not prepared to admit it. The cool wine would soothe her burning mouth and lend a touch of civilisation to the proceedings.

Her mind in turmoil, she watched Nik as his steady hand poured the drinks.

'Yassou.' In a parody of friendship his glass clinked hers as she remained silent.

'Of course,' he resumed their conversation as if there had been no traumatic interruption, settling down in an adjacent chair, 'Markos has no idea of who you are, and for the time being that's how it must remain. If and when the time is right he may be told, but I shall be the best judge of that. Is that agreed?'

For Markos's sake it was the best solution. Despite the prickly antagonism she still felt against Nik, even Karis could see that. 'Agreed,' she concurred shortly. 'By the way, who is Tonia?'

'Antonia is my housekeeper's niece. Her family live in Ierapetra and when she's on vacation from university she keeps an eye on Markos when required.'

'And Nikoletta? Is she your housekeeper?'

'Nikoletta?' Nik gave a short humourless laugh. 'It's difficult to imagine Nikoletta in the role of a housekeeper. She'd be as amazed as Markos if someone told her mashed potato could be pink!' For a brief second a smile chased the wintry look from his stern face before he continued slowly, 'I might as well tell you, since I imagine someone else will do if I don't. Nikoletta is the woman most people expected me to marry. Shall we go down to dinner now?'

'Why not?' Karis rose to her feet, smoothing the soft silk of her skirt, wishing she dared ask whether she was likely to meet his Greek girlfriend, whether she and Nik had been lovers—if they still intended to be lovers—and knowing she dared not: that it was none of her business and she had no right to care one way or the other. Unfortunately, for some inexplicable reason, she did!

Dinner gave her a chance to unwind, certain as she was that her husband's volatile temper would be well under control in a public place where he was so well known. The dining-room, as she had supposed, was magnificent, the meal excellent and the Greek wine and brandy of the premier class. Nik was charming and attentive, as befitted a man on his honeymoon, telling her more about the environs of Ierapetra where they would be staying as well as conversing on more general things. Watching his animated face as he recounted a droll episode in his own childhood when he had gone out in mask and flippers hunting octopus and actually discovered one, Karis found herself unexpectedly warming to his personality. For the first time he was showing her a facet of his nature she had never guessed existed—one she was finding undeniably attractive.

How wise she had been to express a wish to dine in public, she congratulated herself smugly as the waiter cleared the small dish from which she had eaten her crème caramel, only to gasp in horror the next moment as the lights of the room were dimmed and a disembodied voice announced to everyone that they were honoured by the presence of the hotel's executive director—Nikolaos Christianides—and his new wife on their wedding day.

Amidst a chorus of shouts and good wishes and a round of applause, the head waiter appeared wheeling before him an iced and decorated wedding cake set on an internally illuminated stand.

'From the staff and guests, with affection and good wishes,' he intoned solemnly, setting the trolley before them.

Wishing the floor would open and swallow her up, Karis stared down at her hands, an embarrassed flush climbing her cheeks.

'My wife and I are overwhelmed by your kindness and generosity, which, as you see, has taken us completely by surprise.' Nik was on his feet, his deep voice calmly composed. 'We invite you all to share the cake and participate in our happiness.'

'Go on, give her a kiss!' It was an English voice which pierced the hum of conversation as the lights rose to their former brilliance and the waiter began his task of dividing the iced edifice before him. To Karis's consternation the cry was taken up by another tourist and repeated by two others—'What are you waiting for? Kiss the bride!'

She cringed as Nik's arm slid beneath her elbow, relentlessly forcing her to rise. 'You know what they say,' he murmured. 'The customer's always right—and however ill-advised your countrymen, they do mean well.'

Faced with the inevitable, Karis put as brave a face as possible on it, closing her eyes and lifting her cheek for Nik's peck. Instead it was her soft mouth he sought with his warm lips, brushing their surface with a slow, sensuous movement as different from their previous assault as it was possible to be. Between her shoulderblades, sensitive fingers splayed and pressured as, unbelievably, Karis felt her breasts beneath the thin silk sear with an inner fire. Just when her body clamoured for more, the caress was finished, the cheers subsiding and normal conversation resuming. Grateful to be out of the spotlight, she resumed her seat, nibbling at her own small portion of cake, questioning her tumultuous feelings. Nik had put on a fine act for an appreciative audience, so why had it left her feeling so empty and defeated?

After the meal ended, feigning a deeper weariness than she felt, she was glad to escape to her designated bedroom, leaving Nik collating reports for the next day's meeting. It was two in the morning when she awakened remembering the spray of freesia still in her bag. With a small cry of annoyance she slid from the bed, located the bag and rescued the wilting spray from its depth. The flowers were definitely jaded, but not beyond recall. In seconds she had made her way to the large, marble-fitted bathroom, helped herself to a toothglass and, separating the stalks from their silver foil packing, plunged them into the water.

'What's the matter? Are you ill?' To her horror Nik appeared at the entrance to the lobby, still fully dressed, his brow creased into a frown.

'No, I'm fine.' Suddenly aware of the picture she must make in her burgundy silk nightdress with its deep V-neckline edged with écru lace, Karis held the glass of freesias against her thundering heart. Glamorous nightwear was one of her weaknesses—a defence against the trim, tailored dresses she had to wear for work. But what would Nik think to see her garbed like a siren, the shape and colour of her flesh gleaming through the flimsy covering?

He looked tired, dark shadows beneath his eyes, lines of strain bisecting his cheeks, but his eyes retained their brilliance, dwelling on the glass of flowers in her hand. There was something in those eyes that alarmed her, sent frissons of apprehension through her limbs. It was difficult to speak, her voice sounding husky and unreal as she found the words she wanted.

'What about you, Nik? Why are you still dressed? Shouldn't you be in bed?'

'I couldn't sleep, and I have work to do.' He ran a hand through his dark hair, his tone brusque and unfriendly.

'Is there anything I can do?' A wave of compassion passed over her. He must be exhausted! 'Make you a cup of coffee, perhaps?'

'For pity's sake, Karis!' The harshness of his reply assaulted her. 'This is a first-class hotel. If I want anything I can ring room service for it—anything at all! There's nothing you can do but get back to bed, shut your door and leave me to get on with my work!'

So much for the gentleness she'd thought she had detected in him over dinner! She obeyed him without another word. No one had asked him to come looking for her, had they? Burying her head in the soft pillow, she forced herself to forget Nik and to think of Markos instead. In minutes she was asleep again, the sweet scent of freesias perfuming her dreams.

CHAPTER SIX

'YOU HAVEN'T forgotten that tonight we have to attend my father's name-day party?' Nik demanded sharply the following morning, finishing his second croissant and fixing Karis with a commanding look that dared her to contest his reminder.

'Of course not. Where is it being held, and what time do we have to be there?' She refilled his coffee-cup, inwardly amused at her own prompt acceptance of a wifely role.

'Here, in the Crystal Ballroom.' Nik accepted his replenished cup with a curt nod of thanks. 'As to time—well, if he were at home it would go on from dawn until the following daybreak, but, since he's chairing the conference, any time from eight this evening onwards will be acceptable. I assume you bought yourself a suitable dress as I requested—may I see it, please?'

There was nothing in the pleasant tenor of his request to suggest he had no confidence in her choice, but how else could she take it? Conscious that the sleeveless, V-necked royal blue silk chiffon ankle-length sheath, its drapes radiating from the midriff, its front skirt split from the knee to hem for easy walking, appeared deceptively plain and simple on a hanger, she nevertheless presented it to Nik without a word of explanation in its favour.

He surveyed it with narrowed eyes and pursed lips. 'This is your idea of seductive?' he asked coolly at last.

'You said seductive, not flashy,' Karis responded crisply. 'I assumed you didn't want me to wear anything blatantly sexy.'

'Neither did I wish it to appear that you were wearing your nightdress! Although . . .' surprisingly there was a gleam amusement in his dark eyes, 'on second thoughts, the nightdress you were wearing last night would certainly be an attention-getter.' He raised his hand to finger the delicate material thoughtfully. 'On second thoughts, the fabric is superb. It may be exactly right to gild the lily with such simplicity. The colour too is quite perfect.'

Perfect for what? she wondered as Nik rose leisurely to his feet. She supposed it was natural he would want his father to approve of his new wife. From the little she knew of Andriana, she was going to be a hard act to follow. Well, whatever Nik's reservations might still be, once he saw the way the dress followed the lines of her body, flowing lovingly over its curves but never giving them undue prominence, she hoped he would be finally persuaded that her choice had been right.

Left to her own devices for the day after Nik's departure, Karis, dressed casually in cream denims and a dark brown T-shirt, refreshed her memory with the streets and shops of Iraklion, walking through the fruit market savouring the sight and smell of exotic produce and enjoying the sights in some of the quiet back streets where artisans still went about their own businesses of leather work, carpentry and shoemaking. The late April weather was fine and warm, and she lunched pleasurably on a kiosk-bought cheese pie, sitting in one of the city parks enjoying her environment, trying to prepare herself for the ordeals ahead of her.

With her appetite satiated and her mind and body refreshed, she decided to spend the afternoon in the Iraklion Museum, visiting her favourite exhibits, experiencing the same thrill of pleasure she always had in their presence: the magnificent golden-horned rhyton in the form of a bull's head, the legendary 'Snake Goddess'— the faience figurine who was surely the precursor of all the topless lady sunbathers on the Cretan beaches in modern times, the translucent rock crystal vase unearthed at Zakros . . . The treasures of the past, so beautifully crafted, never failed to give her a deep sense of satisfaction.

If anything was likely to make the hours pass more quickly then this was it, she thought, passing from the golden double-headed axes of ritual to gaze in admiration at the famous honey-bee pendant, intricately worked and worn by a Minoan queen more than a thousand years before the birth of Christ.

Inevitably it was the jewellery that fascinated her more than anything—the necklaces taken from the tombs of Phaistos, composed of beads of semi-precious stones, amethyst, cornelian, steatite, spherical or amygdaloid, and the fabulous gold ring from Isopata with the cult scene on its ovoid bezel.

Sighing, she tore herself away from the showcase, acknowledging that it was here, some six years previously, that the seeds of her interest in jewellery had been sown. She sighed. So much of her life had been influenced by this country—it was inevitable she would return.

It was late afternoon when she returned to the hotel, to find the suite still empty. Taking her time, Karis prepared herself for the evening ahead, enjoying a long, luxurious bath before smoothing perfumed body foam into every inch of her skin, savouring its subtle, elusive scent as she slipped into the silk one-piece bodyshaper which was the only possible garment to wear beneath her new dress.

Nik returned just as she was leaving the bathroom. Glad she had had the forethought to cover herself in the silk wrap which matched her nightdress, Karis asked politely about his day.

'We got a lot of work completed,' he told her, flexing his broad shoulders, as if to shift the burdens of the day. 'My father was in fine style—a little surprised at the suddenness of our marriage perhaps, but expressing a keen interest in meeting you.'

'I hope he won't be disappointed.' For a moment anxiety showed in her frown.

'I'm afraid I've continually disappointed him.' Nik's smile bordered on the malicious as she felt her heart sink. 'But don't let that worry you, Karis *mou*, because I can assure you it won't worry me!'

With that hardly reassuring statement he went into the bathroom and shortly afterwards she heard the shower running. Damn Giorgios Christianides! she thought viciously, brushing her red-brown curls with unnecessary vigour. What was it about her likely to win his disapproval—her nationality? Her previous occupation as a shopgirl? Deliberately she downgraded her former occupation as the elder Christianides might. Had he wanted Nik to marry the mysterious Nikoletta? Perhaps the other girl was a real beauty and the two of them would have made as pretty a pair as their names. Well, it wasn't to be, and Nik at least had vowed he wasn't going to be daunted by his father's reception of her, so why should she worry?

Yet she *was* concerned as she surveyed herself in the full-length mirror of her bedroom. She was Markos's mother, and one day that fact was going to be known. For his sake alone she wanted to be accepted by Nik's family. Satisfied at last that there was nothing further she could do to improve her appearance, she took a deep breath, straightened her shoulders and went to confront Nik.

'Exquisite!' His reception was everything that she had hoped for and more. 'I withdraw my earlier reservations wholeheartedly. Your taste is impeccable.'

The unstinted acclamation brought the colour to her cheeks as Nik came towards her, lifting her hands and holding her away from him, critical eyes absorbing every detail of her toilette from her tumble of mahogany hair to the pointed toes of her royal blue satin stiletto court shoes. Formally dressed in the pale fawn lightweight suit he had worn to their wedding, Nik himself looked magnificent, Karis registered, experiencing an unexpected tremor of excitement at the feel of his hard palm against her own.

'But you won't need a wristwatch.' His dark head bent over her wrist as he unlatched the gold cocktail watch that graced it, ignoring the small murmur of protest she made. 'I will tell you when it's time to leave, and besides, I have something for you that will be more becoming to your lovely arm.' Reaching into an inside pocket, Nik produced a faded velvet jeweller's box, placing it in one of her upturned palms. 'Open it, Karis. Tell me if you like it.'

Speechlessly she obeyed him, her mouth forming a silent 'Oh' as she stared down at a gold bracelet set with three rows of precious stones—diamonds and sapphires, in an identical arrangement to the ring she had chosen in London.

'Nik!' Words continued to fail her as she lifted it from its bed of crushed satin. Her practised eye told her immediately that she was looking at not only a very beautiful piece of jewellery but one that was worth thousands of pounds.

'It was my mother's,' Nik said unemotionally as he took it from her hand and clasped it round her bare wrist. 'She bequeathed it to me in her will. These go with it.'

The second box he produced contained sapphire and diamond drop earrings. 'As soon as I saw your dress I knew the time had come to let you wear them,' he told her casually, as with a flash of understanding she realised why he had asked only to see diamond and sapphire rings back in London. 'Would you like me to fix them for you?' He tipped the glittering jewels into her hand.

Suddenly she was all fingers and thumbs, as she slid her own golden sleepers from her small neat lobes. 'I—I'm not sure. Can you?'

For answer he took her to one of the chairs, indicating that she be seated before perching on the arm himself.

Strange that such large masculine hands should be so gentle and precise, that the delicate fastenings should respond so easily to Nik's direction. In seconds the tantalising fall of precious stones swung against her neck, but more tantalising still was the closeness of Nik's presence: the faint evocative scent of his aftershave, the warm, arousing aroma of his skin and hair. Suddenly Karis was too aware of the nearness of his mouth to her own and the strange, unwelcome yearning she felt for his kiss.

This would never do! She was allowing herself to be drawn into a fantasy of her own making, and it had to stop. Nothing had changed between them and never would. Nik had had one love in his life and his heart had been buried with her . . . That was something she must never forget.

Resolutely Karis pushed herself to her feet, teetering a little in her unaccustomed high heels. 'I really do appreciate your letting me wear these . . .' Briefly she touched her wrist and ears. 'They must awaken memories you'd rather forget—your mother, Andriana . . .'

She stopped abruptly as his brow darkened. It had been tactless to mention his wife. She should have known better than to remind him, yet with Andriana's jewels on her body she felt so guilty to be alive when the woman who had loved and befriended her son wasn't.

'Andriana never wore them,' Nik said curtly, staring up at her, his jaw taut. 'She was a gentle, quiet girl who found no pleasure in dressing up and partying. As for my mother—she hated them. They represented my father's cupidity when all she really wanted was his fidelity. So you see, they have no sentimental value at all for me. Tonight they merely reinforce what everyone present already knows—that Nikolaos Christianides can afford to buy whichever woman he wants.' Open hostility gleamed in his black eyes now as he rose to his full height, causing Karis to take a faltering step away from him, so powerful was the sense of his displeasure. 'So please don't read more into their loan than there is. Tomorrow they go back into the bank. Now, if you're ready, shall we go and dazzle Papa with your beauty?'

The Crystal Ballroom, hung with the sparkling chandeliers from which it derived its name, was already full of people when they entered. A long table was set out with a variety of foods, while at the far end a bar, stretched along the full width of the large room, appeared to be doing brisk business. Small tables and chairs were attractively placed in groups while to one side the thick plush carpet finished to give place to a fair-sized dance floor at the far side of which a bouzouki band was playing.

Karis's gaze skimmed across the dancers already moving to the romantic strains of some popular Greek music, seeking her host. Dismissing the small groups of mixed couples sitting at the tables or standing in desultory conversation, her eyes fastened on a gathering of half a dozen men positioned by the bar, the centre of whose attention was a tall, broad figure whose greying hair did nothing to detract from the vitality of his bearing.

She felt Nik's hand tighten on her arm as across the length of the room the roving alert eyes of the tall figure found and fastened on her, then flicked their hard glance to Nik before returning once more to focus on her alone. She had been right in her recognition.

As if by magic the people standing between them seemed to move away; even the group surrounding Giorgios melted, leaving Nik and herself alone in his boldly assessing gaze.

A lazy arm curled loosely round her waist as, obeying the unspoken command, Nik led her towards the waiting figure of his father.

'*Hronia pola!*' It was the younger man who broke the silence with the formal name-day greeting of 'Many Happy Returns'. 'I have the honour to present my wife, Karis, to you, Papa.'

Beneath the stern regard turned on her Karis lifted her small chin proudly. She had no need to quail beneath that dark, shrewd appraisal—and she had no intention of doing so either, however formidable the elder Christianides!

'*Na ta ekatostisis!*' she murmured politely, thinking how apt the greeting was. Here was a man who would undoubtedly greet his hundredth celebration with the same verve and style she recognised today. The sense of power emanating from him was almost tangible. It was easy to see the source of Nik's aggressive genes!

'Ah—you speak our language!' The heavy face broke into a smile. 'A fact you forgot to mention at our brief talk this morning, *yiós mou.*' He cast a mildly accusing look at the younger man.

'Because I believed you to be more interested in her qualities of domesticity and fecundity than her linguistic attributes,' Nik riposted softly. 'You will find my wife is talented in many fields. Her ability with languages is only a small portion of her accomplishments.'

'Indeed? Then I must congratulate you doubly. Beauty and brains are a formidable combination in a

woman—and a dangerous one!' Giorgios's eyes dropped
speculatively from Karis's face to settle contemplatively
on the circle of jewels around her wrist, as if their
presence there surprised him.

Karis felt the hairs on the back of her neck stiffen.
Father and son were like two lions facing up to each other,
mutual admiration and distrust positive emotions
running between them. Uncomfortably she sensed the
strength of the complex bond between the two men,
intuitively knowing it wasn't based on love but some
darker emotion she could only guess at.

'Forewarned is forearmed,' Nik's smile was for her
alone, a mischievous twist of his mouth, which made her
heart leap as she credited him with being a good actor.

'Then I must welcome you to our family.' Giorgios
paused to assess Karis coolly, his gaze blatant but not
insolent. 'As my son's wife you must regard my family,
my house and my support as your own.'

'Thank you.' She accepted the formal offer gracefully,
allowing the older man to take her hand and raise it with
studied courtesy to his lips.

It hadn't been such an ordeal after all, she thought with
relief as Nik led her across to join the crowd at the main
table.

It was much later after they had eaten and drunk that
Karis found herself held tightly against Nik's body on the
dance floor, moving slowly to the gentle rhythm of the
bouzoukis.

Every nerve cell of her body was registering his
closeness, her body adapting itself to the hard male
outlines of his. They were dancing much too close for her
peace of mind, yet she couldn't find the courage or the
willpower to pull herself away.

When Nik's lips caressed her forehead, brushing
against her ear as he eased her soft form even more

intimately against himself, she knew it was an act to impress his fellow guests, so there was no logical explanation for the havoc it caused inside her, the warm flood of feeling that was moving her to a high pitch of receptivity. So she was greatly relieved when the music was halted, the lights dimmed and an announcement made that Florina Stavrolakes was about to entertain them with a performance of *ribetico*.

As Karis allowed Nik to guide her to a seat, three bouzouki players from the band sat round in a circle on the raised dais to be joined by a woman, whom Karis judged to be in her late thirties or early forties. Slim and beautiful, her black hair drawn back from an oval face in which the eyes were the most remarkable feature, her appearance was greeted with a warm round of applause. Dressed in a long, close-fitting black sequin-decorated dress, she stood holding tightly to the back rail of a chair. The bouzoukis played and she began to sing.

Despite her stay in Crete, Karis had never heard *ribetico* sung, knowing it only as being totally different from folk music; better described perhaps as soul music, its roots in poverty, deprivation, injustice and shattered dreams. Now, as Florina Stavrolakes's thrilling voice filled the atmosphere, she felt its power for herself, absorbing through her senses the same aching qualities of emotion that coloured the New Orleans blues, the Portuguese *fado*, and the Spanish *canto jondo*.

The Greek woman sang with the strength, depth and magic of an Edith Piaf, her voice raw yet tuneful, deep but feminine, incredibly moving. Giorgios's guests sat spellbound as the cigarette smoke spiralled in a blue haze to the ceiling and that poignantly beautiful voice sobbed out its tales of life and love: of longing and losing.

Swallowing back her too-easily-evoked tears, Karis glanced at Nik's profile, feeling a surge of compassion at the solemnity and sensitivity so disarmingly displayed on the face she had grown to think of as hard.

'She's magnificent!' she declared enthusiastically as the singer accepted the applause following her final rendering. 'Why, Nik, she's so good she could be a professional!'

'She was,' came the dry response. 'Up until ten years ago her name was a household word in Greece.'

'But what happened? Why did she stop?' Visions of some personal tragedy spilled over in Karis's imagination.

'Because my father wasn't prepared to share her talents with an audience not of his choosing. You see, for the past decade she's been his mistress. Now she sings only for his pleasure.'

'Oh!' For a moment she was stunned. 'Then you and she . . .?' She hesitated delicately, giving Nik the opportunity of expressing his feelings.

He gave a short laugh. 'We regard each other with mutual respect, since we are the only two people around who have enjoyed any long-term relationship with him! Come, I'll introduce you to her. I think you'll like her.'

'My dear, I'm so happy for both of you!' Florina's smile was wide and generous as Nik made his excuses and left them within a few minutes of their introduction to return to the bar. 'Nik has been through a terrible time and I'm afraid Giorgios's ultimatums only made things harder for him. Thank goodness he met you when he did, so we can all get back to normal again!'

'Giorgios's ultimatums?' Karis queried, totally at a loss. 'What do you mean?'

'You didn't know?' For a few seconds Florina looked distressed. 'Then please forgive me for speaking out of turn. I suppose I assumed that Nik would have told you and you'd both had a good laugh at them.' She shrugged her shoulders. 'As if Nik would have taken any notice of them anyway! You'd think after everything that's happened Giorgios would recognise his own stubbornness manifested in his own flesh and blood!'

A feeling of deep unease engulfed Karis. 'Nik's father didn't want him to marry me?' she asked anxiously. 'He had other plans for him? Is that it? Nikoletta, perhaps?'

'Good heavens, no, my dear!' Florina gave her forearm a friendly squeeze. 'It was nothing personal. It's true he would have been happy to see Nikoletta as his daughter-in-law. Nik and she have been friendly for the past two years, besides which she owns a chain of fashion boutiques and Giorgios would have enjoyed seeing those come under Christianides control. He has an acquisitive nature!' She paused to take another long sip from the glass in her hand. 'The problem was that Nik seemed in no haste to remarry, and his father was afraid he might settle for the life of a widower.'

'Would that have been so dreadful?' Karis asked, surprised. It seemed a strange attitude for Giorgios Christianides to take, particularly when it appeared he had made precisely the same decision after his own wife's death.

'Oh, yes.' Florina's magnificent dark eyes held Karis's puzzled appraisal. 'To Giorgios it would have been a tragedy. He was desperate for Nik to remarry and beget an heir to the family fortune!'

'But Nik already has an heir,' Karis interjected, her eyebrows winging upwards in surprise.

'Ah, little Markos, you mean.' Florina sighed. 'Of course you know he's adopted? Poor Andriana couldn't have children, and I'm afraid Giorgios has never accepted the child as his grandson.' She took another long sip from the glass she held in her hand as Karis recognised the unmistakable aroma of Metaxa. 'When he discovered that Andriana could never become a mother he actually wanted Nik to divorce her, because he was so set on perpetuating the family line into the twenty-first century: but of course Nik wouldn't hear of it. Instead he adopted poor little Markos, but all that served to do, I'm afraid, was to alienate Giorgios even more. He took it as a personal affront that Nik should give the family name to some abandoned bastard.'

A light laugh came from her soft, sensuous mouth. 'But you won't want to hear all this family gossip—particularly since it's all over and done with. Nik has fallen in love again and the continuation of the Christianides line is ensured, which means that both you and I have good reason to be happy, my dear!'

'Florina—please—I do want to hear more!' It was as if an icy hand had seized Karis's heart, her emotions uttering a silent scream at the contemptuous description bestowed on her son. Her mind unable to grasp the implications of what she had already heard, only her heart warned her that she might have been terribly misled by Nik's vaunted concern for her child.

As Giorgios's mistress shook her head doubtfully, Karis touched her free hand impulsively, clasping the palm as she pleaded. 'Obviously, from what you've just said, it's important to you as well that Nik has married again. The more I know about the background, the more likely I am to be able to make our marriage succeed!' As the older woman continued to look doubtful, Karis insisted passionately, 'I want to know what ultimatums Giorgios could possibly have laid down! What exactly did he use as an inducement?'

'My dear girl,' Florina cast her an amused look, 'Anyone seeing you together tonight will know you're in love with each other, so your marriage will automatically succeed! Whatever their faults, the Christianides men have a natural aptitude for the art of love . . .'

For a brief moment Karis was distracted from her own problems by the naked suffering apparent on the other woman's face. Damn all men for their selfishness and abuse of a woman's emotions! she thought with an untypical burst of venom, before continuing to plead.

'Florina . . . please?' she begged. 'It's important for me to know.'

'If you insist, then . . .' The Greek woman paused, assessing the determination on her face, then asked quietly, 'I assume Nik told you about the relationship I have with his father?' At Karis's nod she went on softly, 'Well, the truth of the matter is that after Andriana died, Giorgios told Nik that unless he remarried as soon as the period of mourning was over and had his own children, he, Giorgios, would pre-empt him: marry again, beget himself another heir and disown Nik completely.' She shrugged her shoulders philosophically. 'Giorgios and I have a satisfying relationship, but I'm too old to have children, so in the event of Nik remaining unmarried, I would have lost the man I've lived with and loved for the past ten years. That is why, tonight, I have cause to celebrate!'

Horrified, Karis stared at the older woman, her thoughts in turmoil. 'But—but does Nik need his father's patronage? I mean, to the extent of marrying to ensure it?'

'Oh, my dear, no, of course not!' Florina looked as horrified as Karis felt. 'I didn't intend to imply that, only to illustrate how stubborn and intransigent Giorgios can be in family matters! At the present time both he and Nik hold twenty-six per cent of the company shares, which gives them jointly a controlling interest. But whatever Giorgios does, Nik will always retain his own twenty-six per cent, so you are quite correct. Nik is a rich man in his own right. It is Giorgios, not Nik, who sees the world only in terms of drachmas and dollars!'

But Nik was an ambitious man! Karis was as aware of that fact as his father must have been. As Giorgios's heir Nik would wield supreme power in the boardroom, even as he shared it now. Disinherited, his twenty-six per cent could easily be outvoted. And how would he regard a stepmother and a half-brother conceived with the sole purpose of disinheriting him? Pride alone must surely have driven him to oppose such an event? Which meant his father's threat must have carried some weight with him? Spurred him to consider matrimony much earlier than he might otherwise have done?

Feeling faint with shock at the unexpected revelations, Karis searched Florina's face for any signs of malicious satisfaction at the bombshell she had delivered—and found none. Only a deep misery shone in the depths of the other woman's lustrous eyes.

Little wonder she was able to render so admirably the haunting songs of the city streets, Karis accorded silently to herself. To express suffering so exquisitely, one had to have suffered, and loving a man like Giorgios Christianides must be hell! Loving a man like Nik Christianides would be hell too—thank heaven she was too aware of the danger to fall into that trap!

Whatever her husband's motives, it seemed they were more complicated than the simple story he had told her—that of merely wanting a mother for his adopted son, for the child's sake alone!

Watching his tall figure progressing through the crowds towards her, she felt unbearably lonely and threatened, but when he invited her to dance to the renewed strains of the bouzoukis she went into his arms, aware that this was neither the time nor the place to confront him with her growing doubts and fears.

It was much later that night when, near exhaustion from dancing and socialising, Karis found peace and quiet in her own room. Stretching her weary bones on the comfortable mattress, she tried to force her tired mind to evaluate what she had learned from Florina. Of course Nik had refused to divorce Andriana. Everyone knew how much he had loved her! But the promise of total board control on Giorgios's death must have been a powerful lure to him, and one he wouldn't easily turn his broad back on.

Florina had assumed Nik had fallen in love with her, which would have explained everything. Only *she* knew how false an assumption that was! Nik had no intention of taking her to his bed, no intention of siring the legitimate children his father wanted. So why had he married her? Something there didn't ring true. Her tired brain sought a solution and found none. Unless—on the point of sleep an idea came—perhaps he meant to punish his father for his outrageous suggestion of divorce by making the older man wait in vain for the grandchildren he wanted, while presenting a front of obedience to prevent him from taking the extreme action he had threatened.

It was a cruel and cold-blooded revenge and, although deserved, somehow unworthy of the man she had married. Then finally, as she saw the situation through Nik's eyes, a dreadful suspicion arose. He had loved Andriana, *did* love the child they had both adopted, and meeting her, Karis, once more he had seen a way to ensure that Markos received his grandfather's recognition.

Her husband was going to await his moment, then he would tell Giorgios Christianides that she, Karis, was Markos's mother—and he himself the father whom she had refused to name. It was simple and perfect, explained so many things which had been mysteries, and there was no one alive to dispute it—except herself.

Sleep driven from her mind, she sat up in bed, hugging her arms around herself as she shivered. Naturally Nik would expect her co-operation. On the surface it seemed she would have every reason to support the fraud, for that was what it amounted to, but she wouldn't . . . couldn't, even to ensure Markos's eventual inheritance of the Christianides empire. Yanis had lived so briefly, loved so fleetingly, but he deserved more than for his memory to be obliterated, his flesh and blood accredited to another man to punish an intractable and arrogant patriarch, however rich the rewards of that deception would be!

She must discover, urgently, if she had guessed Nik's intentions correctly, and if so, as soon as the opportunity offered itself she would tell him how she felt—that she would never agree to them!

CHAPTER SEVEN

THERE was obviously not going to be an opportunity to broach the matter the following morning as Karis joined Nik for breakfast in the lounge. Neither was she sure how she was going to introduce it, but it was obvious she would need more time than Nik was prepared to give her now as he thumbed through a sheaf of papers in preparation for the morning's conference session.

In fact they had exchanged nothing more than the formal pleasantries of strangers sharing the same table by the time he gathered up his briefcase and left the room.

How the hours were dragging before the reunion for which she was longing! Karis took the photograph of Markos from her handbag and gazed at the child's face, feeling a warm rush of maternal love flowing through every cell of her body. Whatever Nik's motives, surely he could do nothing now to prevent her from holding her son in her arms? But caution warned her it might be prudent to wait a few days before confronting her husband with her suspicions.

Reluctantly she returned the photograph to the security of her bag. There was no point in sitting around dwelling on her problems; she must find something to do to make the hours pass more quickly.

It only took a few minutes to get herself ready to leave the hotel. Today, in deference to the early spring warmth, she would wear a summer dress. Selecting a pale blue cotton with short sleeves and a tailored neckline, she belted her narrow waist with a chocolate-coloured belt, slipping her feet into smart low-heeled casuals perfect for a day's walking round a city. Gathering her purse, make-up bag and tissues in a soft shoulder-bag that matched her belt, she made for the street, leaving her key at the desk as she passed.

By lunchtime she had visited the cathedral, spent a pleasant hour or so window-shopping and found herself back in the centre of the city. At half-past twelve Morosini Square was packed. Standing, her back to the Fountain of the Lions, Karis watched the bustling scene with deep remembered pleasure. Completely pedestrianised, the centre of the road was filled with tables, brightly clothed beneath the dappled shade of the overhanging trees.

The narrow pavement each side was shared by strolling tourists, dashing waiters holding loaded trays aloft and the inevitable *kamaki*—the young men on the prowl for female companionship. She smiled to herself, appreciating the humour of the way the Greek word for spear-fishing was used idiomatically in this entirely different but graphic context.

Casting her eyes over the scene in front of her, she tried to discern a vacant place at one of the tables. If she stood there much longer she would become a target for the *kamaki* herself! Of course she didn't have to eat at Morosini—there were plenty of other restaurants and tavernas in the locality, but this central rendezvous with its mix of locals and tourists would provide a welcome diversion.

A pang of sadness twisted in her heart as she recalled that it had been Yanís who had described Morosini as being 'full of tourists rushing about trying to get the seats the Greeks already occupied!' It had been an acknowledgement of the fact that a Greek spent a great deal longer over a cup of coffee than most Englishmen did over a four-course meal! A fact that was of no comfort to her at all at that moment.

'Karis?'

The sound of her name spoken in a deep masculine timbre at close quarters brought her sharply back to the present. Startled, she turned to face a slimly built man about her own height and age. Even after six years there was no mistaking him.

'Dimitri!' she exclaimed, her eyes sparkling with joy. 'Oh, Dimitri—how wonderful to see you again!'

Impulsively she held out her hands to the man who had been Yanís's best friend and her own companion on so many occasions in the past. The two young men had been casual friends before she had come into Yanís's life. Strangely, against the odds, her arrival had intensified their friendship, breeding into it a deep loyalty. On the nights when Yanís had been working late and Dimitri had been free, the former had entrusted her to his friend to be her escort. It had been a trust Dimitri had never abused.

Now he took both her hands in his own, his eyes drawn to the rings on her finger. 'I could hardly believe my eyes when I saw you standing here like a ghost from the past.' His voice softened. 'I thought I must be hallucinating. You're married too, I see.' He raised enquiring eyebrows. 'And you've brought your husband back to Crete on a holiday?'

'No,' she dimpled, knowing she was going to surprise him. 'It's the other way round. He brought me back—you see, Nik's Greek.'

'Aha—the English girls always did have impeccable taste!' A grin split his face.

'So did the Greek boys,' she teased him. 'Do you and your friends still spend your Sundays admiring the topless tourists on the beach?'

'Beauty always deserves its due!' His eyes lingered on her animated face. 'You're even more lovely than you used to be.' It was a connoisseur's gaze that surveyed her. 'Thinner, I think, but your nose is still as perfect, your mouth still as beautiful, and as for your glorious hair . . .'

'Dimitri!' she protested laughingly, flattered but embarrassed by his personal assessment.

He shrugged his shoulders. 'A compliment to a friend, Karis,' he told her easily. 'I won't give your husband cause for jealousy.'

Before she could reply, he dropped her hands to take her lightly by the elbow. 'Let me give you lunch at my taverna.'

'You own your own taverna?' It had always been his dream. 'Here, in Morosini?' Her delight for his success shone in her face as he nodded his head.

'My cousins and I are partners.'

'Then I shall certainly let you give me a meal, for old times' sake.'

She followed him through the spread of tables and chairs, stopping with unfeigned pleasure when they reached the Minerva Taverna and Dimitri ushered her into a newly vacated seat at a table for two, sitting down to join her.

Looking around her, Karis swallowed the lump in her throat, memories flooding back to her. It had been here one evening that the three of them, Yanís, Dimitri and herself, had come after visiting a disco. They had had little money between them, ending up by sharing one large pizza. It was then that Dimitri had vowed that one day he would own the place and eat his way through the menu . . .

'I tried to get in touch with you again.' His voice broke into her recollections. 'After Yanís's accident, I mean. When I'd finished my training I came back to Crete and asked at the hotel, but the management had changed and no one knew where you were. I assumed you'd returned to England.'

Karis nodded. 'It was such a dreadful shock—such a wasted life . . .' She stared at the table as a young waiter replaced the soiled linen. And it had been Dimitri himself who had broken the news to her. Of course, being away in the Peloponnese with Yanís at the time, he had had no idea that she'd been carrying his friend's child. With Elizabeth and her family moved to the mainland, where she had gradually lost touch with them, it was doubtful if Dimitri had ever learned about her becoming a mother. It was something she resolved not to tell him; it could only complicate the complex situation she was already in.

'Yes.' She wasn't imagining the tears in the Greek's eyes as his hand touched hers across the table and she felt his compassion. 'His parents left the island, you know,' he added. 'With the compensation they received from the Government they bought an olive farm on the mainland.'

'Did they?' That figured. How ironic that Yanís's ambition had always been to buy a farm for his parents—at least in death he had achieved that! Abruptly Karis picked up the menu.

'I must warn you, I'm starving!' she announced with forced gaiety, tearing her mind away from the tragedy of the past.

'Good!' Dimitri followed her lead. 'I shan't be content till you've sampled the best we can offer you, and while you're eating I want to know everything that's happened to you since last we met.'

It was some five hours later that Karis sank down gracefully into the soft upholstery of Dimitri's car.

'Tired?' he enquired laconically.

'A little,' she agreed, smothering a yawn. 'But it's been a lovely afternoon.'

After lunch Dimitri had persuaded her to revisit the small beach settlement where they had first met. In six years there had been few changes. Apart from the hotel being under new management the taverna where Yanís had worked had changed hands too, but the shops along the beach were the same, the sand still as white and soft, the curving bay still as inviting as it had ever been.

They had sat in the warm spring sunshine, talking with pleasure about the past, until the temperature had dropped, reminding them of the imminence of a cool evening.

'I'm sorry?' Lost in her thoughts, Karis was only vaguely aware that Dimitri had spoken as he started the engine.

He cast her a curious glance, but repeated patiently, 'I said you must bring your husband to the Minerva. I'd be delighted to meet him.'

'Yes, thank you. I'm sure he'd love to come,' she answered politely, knowing it to be a lie, for it was clear Nik despised her previous existence and the friends she had made during it. Turning her face to the window, she gazed out at the panorama of sea as Dimitri took the winding road from the village that after three miles of hairpin bends would bring them to the main highway back to Iraklion.

Raising her hand to her head as the journey progressed, she teased the locks of windblown hair that clustered round her face, realising too that her skin was already beginning to feel warm and tight after its exposure to sea and sun. When she got back to the hotel a shower and shampoo would be a must!

Once in Iraklion she directed Dimitri to the hotel, struggling out of the car as he came round to open the passenger door for her, her skirt rising to the top of her thighs as she stepped on to the pavement, gratefully accepting his arm.

'Too much sun?' he asked sympathetically as she grimaced.

'My fair skin,' she admitted ruefully. 'Not knowing I'd end up on the beach I didn't use suncream, but it's not so bad that an application of yogurt won't cure it!' She smiled up into his pleasant face, not wanting him to think the day had been anything but entirely enjoyable, although he would never know just how much she had needed the company of a compatible friend to take her thoughts away from her own problems!

For a split second they stood looking at each other with the real affection of two people who had shared a common tragedy, then with a spontaneous gesture Dimitri stepped forward to give her a gentle hug, his hard cheek coming to rest for a moment against her own. 'I'm so glad everything worked out well for you—it would be just what Yanís wanted!'

How right he was, Karis thought, a ray of happiness shafting through her, as she collected her key from the desk and entered the lift. How proud her lover would have been of his son, how delighted that she, his mother, would be with Markos as he entered manhood to give him the support and understanding Yanís's own parents had always found beyond them! If only her suspicions of Nik's intentions should prove unfounded . . . if only one day she would be able to persuade him to let her tell Markos about the happy, sensitive boy who had been his father . . .

Entering the empty suite, she flung her bag down on one of the armchairs, walking directly through to her bedroom, slipping her feet out of her shoes, unclasping her belt and lifting her dress over her head. She was on the point of removing the underlying white camisole set on which she had lavished a small fortune at Harrods when she heard the outer door of the suite open and close again forcefully.

Not anticipating that Nik would come directly to her bedroom, she had made no effort to shield her undie-clad body from his eyes as he pushed the door open and confronted her.

'Where have you been?' He was deeply furious. Eyes as adamant and black as jet, the strong lines of his face etched into harsh disfavour, he demanded an answer.

Conscious of her tousled appearance, Karis raked her fingers through dishevelled hair. So she looked untidy, but she didn't deserve the bitter disapproval aimed at her. Nik had left her to her own devices. Surely he hadn't expected her to spend the whole day by herself in the suite?

'I went window-shopping, had lunch in Morosini and spent the rest of the afternoon on the beach,' she told him tersely, seeing no point in elucidating. 'I hadn't realised your meeting was going to finish so early.'

'So I gathered.' He took two steps towards her, his fingers closing with steely strength round her wrists. Angrily she tried to twist away, but it was useless. 'Who with, Karis?' His voice shook. 'Who was the man who brought you back here in his car—and kissed you?'

A cold trickle of pure fear ran down Karis's spine as she closed her eyes, unable to face the fierce rage that burned in the dark intensity of Nik's regard. Deliberately she hadn't mentioned Dimitri, sensing that the time wasn't right to introduce him into the conversation. Now, as her heart sank, she knew her instinct had been faultless. But the conference must have ended early and Nik been in the main hotel lounge overlooking the forecourt as she had said goodbye to Dimitri. Dear heaven, what mischief did he suspect her of now?

'Answer me, damn you!' His voice was vibrantly low and intent, his anger channelled in a narrow stream, every bit of it directed at her. 'Or do I have to beat the truth out of you!'

He looked furious enough to do precisely what he

threatened as every nerve in her body went on edge. Physical violence between a man and woman was something Karis abhorred, something totally outside her experience. If Nik were to lay a finger on her, how could she ever bring herself to live with him? Her face drained of colour. Oh, if only she were able to tell him to go to hell! But the memory of the small face on the photograph told her she must try to take the heat from the situation.

'His name is Dimitri Kasaris.' She tried to keep her voice low and even, but it wasn't easy with Nik towering over her, his aggressive masculinity a potent threat to her welfare.

'Go on.' His keen, penetrating eyes were burning into her, making her feel as if she were suffocating, holding her own gaze by an invisible thread she lacked the strength to dissolve.

She felt his hands tighten on her wrists as if reminding her that it was useless to defy him. For Markos's sake she must endure this cross-examination without losing her temper.

'He's an old friend I met by chance,' she told him levelly. 'He wanted to talk about the past, so after having lunch we went down to the beach for an hour or so. That's all there is to it.' As she stared at his unforgiving face, resentment and fear stiffened her body to automatic defence.

'Is he one of the men who could have been Markos's father?'

Aghast, Karis stared back at his grim face, shocked beyond belief that he could ask such a question.

'Is he, Karis?' Again the question came as a hard muscle jerked spasmodically beneath his cheekbone. 'Damn you, woman—I have to know! Was he one of your lovers?'

'No.' Somehow she managed to speak. 'There was only one man who could have been Markos's father—and he's dead!'

'Dead?' He echoed the word as shock registered on his face. 'How can you know that? Did this Kasaris fellow tell you—or are you still lying?'

'I've never lied to you, Nik,' she said wearily, aware that his grasp had loosened and able now to withdraw her wrist from his hold. 'I told you back in London that I'd always known who the father was but I wasn't able to name him. Now you know why. He was already dead—killed while on exercises during his National Service even before I knew I was expecting his baby.'

There was a short, strained silence as she strove to control the rapid beat of her pulse, and Nik studied her pale face with narrowed eyes. He was the first to break it.

'Presumably your——' he hesitated fastidiously '—your *lover* had parents—a family who would have welcomed their dead son's child, lavished their care and attention on him and you? What was it, selfishness or pride which made you deny them knowledge of their grandchild?' As his dark brows rose in derision it was all Karis could do not to lash out at him with her palm. She looked at his pitiless face, the accusing eyes already determined to disbelieve whatever she would say, and knew she had no option but to try and make him accept what had happened.

'I did go to them,' she said, reliving the anguish of that day. 'They—they called me a liar, turned me away . . .' She saw the disbelief harden on his face, knew how impossible it seemed that a Greek family would turn away their son's child, their dead son's child; but that was the way it had happened, and somehow she must make Nik understand how it had come about.

'You see, they hated me,' she said tonelessly. 'They were peasants, farmers working a tiny smallholding in one of the mountain villages. Yanís was their only son and they'd scraped together what they could so he could have

an education. He was bright and clever and he did well.
At fourteen he left home to work in the tourist tavernas.
He wanted to earn money to see him through his National
Service, but he always sent something back home. Then,
when he fell in love with me, he told them and they were
furious. They refused to meet me or even talk about me.
You see, they wanted him to marry a girl with a land
dowry. It was all they knew—the land . . .'

'Go on,' Nik encouraged her as she paused to gather
her thoughts, his voice as cold and distant as she'd ever
heard it.

'That's it really. Except—they were abusive. They
accused me of alienating Yanís from them, of lying about
our relationship. They said I was after the compensation
the government would pay them, but they'd see I never
got a single drachma . . . that whatever bastard I was
carrying, their son hadn't been the father and they'd
brand me a liar if I dared suggest it.'

'But you were certain he was?' Nik cut a hard gaze
down at her, holding her eyes deliberately as if daring her
to lie.

'Yes,' she answered. 'You see, I believed I loved him.
He was the only one—ever.'

'I see.' Nik's mouth thinned to a grim line. 'And you
never confided in anyone else? You deliberately allowed
everyone to believe you were promiscuous?'

Karis shrugged. 'I had no alternative. To name Yanís
when his parents denied it was to add to their grief. There
was never any hope that they'd accept either me or my
baby. How could I hurt them by making their dead son a
subject of gossip when they were already suffering so
deeply?'

'And the other boys? The ones you associated with so
freely? Do you expect me to believe they never touched
you?'

'I don't expect you to believe anything, Nik.' She looked defiantly into his lean angry face. 'You asked me questions and I've answered them. If you've never been fortunate enough to have friends whom you could trust with your life, your money and your woman then I feel sorry for you. Yanís was a poor man, but in that respect he was much richer than you!'

A hard knot of anger and frustration was burning in her stomach, inciting her to launch herself at the hard implacable face of the man she had married, but she fought down the impulse, trying instead to push her way past him as he barred the exit. She was a fool to think even for one second that he would accept her story!

'And now, if you'll excuse me, I'm tired and sticky, my arms and face are sore from the sun and I want to have a shower.' She was desperately aware of the picture she must make, standing there in the frivolous undies, her face strained and miserable.

'In a moment.' Nik stood four-square in front of her, lifting his hands to rest them gently on her shoulders. 'Do you swear that there is no one on this island who can claim Markos as a relative?'

'Oh!' The monosyllable left her lips and she gave a tormented little shiver as the question penetrated into her numb brain. For a few moments she'd forgotten the plot she suspected Nik of engineering, now it all came back to her. It must be true! That was why he'd been so furious seeing her with Dimitri. If she was still in touch with Markos's biological father, it would have made it much more risky for Nik to have claimed paternity of her son.

'I won't allow it,' she said calmly, watching Nik's handsome face go blank with surprise, and feeling a low coil of triumph uncurl inside her at the thought of thwarting his plans. 'I won't connive to cheat your father. If you don't want Markos's true parentage generally known then I'll abide by that decision, but I absolutely refuse to tell Giorgios that *you* were my lover six years ago!'

'I wasn't aware that I'd asked you to.' The reply was dangerously soft. 'I think you'd better explain yourself, Karis—and fast!'

'Or what?' Her eyes sparkled with blue fire as her battered spirit rose like a phoenix from the ashes of her disillusionment. 'You'll beat me?' Her scathing glance passed from the powerful figure of the man holding her to rest on her own slender body. 'Bravo, Nik!' she said scornfully, and saw his eyes darken ominously.

'There are other ways of subduing a wayward wife, *agapi mou*, and you might suffer more from my hand used to pleasure than punish in your present mood! Now, stop wasting time. I want an explanation.' There was a devilish glint in his dark eyes.

Reminded of the incident at the Acropolis Hotel when Nik had kissed her with a hungry brutality, Karis felt the edge of her opposition dull. She shrugged her shoulders in resignation.

'Florina told me of Giorgios's refusal to accept Markos as his grandson, since he didn't have the Christianides blood in his veins. Thinking about it last night, I came to the conclusion that *that* was why you married me. You thought no one knew who Markos's real father was and that therefore once you produced me as his real mother, you'd be able to claim him for your own. Well, you can't!'

Her voice grew in volume as the anger inside her blossomed. Heedless of the dull flush of fury that rose like a tide on Nik's face, she continued relentlessly, hammering her point home. 'How dare you even think of it? You were a married man at the time, and even if I hadn't been in love with Yanís I would never, *never* have let you make love to me, and I won't allow anyone to believe I would—particularly my son!'

Flushed with righteous indignation, she pushed him hard with both hands, determined this time to reach the bathroom and cool down both her heated body and her temper beneath the shower's cool spray, but Nik was too fast and too strong to be taken off guard.

'Would you not?' he growled. 'And how do you think you would have been able to stop me, if that had been my intention? Any more than you can stop me now?'

She was seized in a relentless grip, her body forced backwards across one of his arms. She fought against him furiously, only to find herself helpless in those hurting, powerful hands, then his parted lips had found hers and she could feel his body taut with passion, feel his heartbeat like muffled thunder against her barely covered breast, as his mouth possessed her with a fierceness that made her tremble. The kiss was ruthless, practised and contemptuous.

She hurt all over when he released her. Her face, her arms, her shins, where the sun had caught her, the muscles in her back, her mouth which had been taken without her permission or co-operation and her heart—yes, most of all her heart, because deep in her subconscious mind she had cherished the thought that the man who had adopted her son had to have more than just a spark of humanity in him—and now that thought had been splintered into fragments.

Nik stood aside and she backed away, her hand rising automatically towards her mouth as if to protect it in retrospect.

'Yes, take your shower, Karis,' he told her curtly, only his own heavy breathing betraying his tightly held emotions. 'You look as if you need it. And since you won't co-operate in cheating my father, as you put it, then I assume you're prepared to collaborate with me in the only possible alternative to ensure my father gets the grandchild he's set his heart on.'

'I don't know what you mean.' But she did, of course she did, and her heart plummeted at the prospect.

The beautiful long-lashed jet-coloured eyes of her husband accorded her a faintly insulting inspection. 'If you hadn't been punished so unkindly by the sun, it would have been my pleasure to demonstrate exactly what I mean at this precise moment. As it is, I suggest you find some lotion to alleviate your discomfort and try and enjoy a good night's sleep.

'As you must be aware by now, the conference finished earlier than expected. Tomorrow morning we leave for Ierapetra, so make the most of your privacy, while you have it. I shall instruct Maria to make up the double room in the villa for us, Karis—so from tomorrow night, whether you like it or not, we shall be living as husband and wife!'

CHAPTER EIGHT

BY MIDDAY Nik's white Mercedes was traversing the narrowest part of the island, through spectacular mountain scenery, towards the south coast. It was a part of the island which remained a mystery to Karis, who during her limited stay there had not strayed far from the northern towns and beaches. While she stared out of the windscreen, appreciating the scenic beauty, her imagination was leaping ahead, envisaging her first meeting with her son. Would he have changed much since the photo she'd seen? Would he really accept her as easily as Nik foresaw?

Since their altercation the previous night she had spoken less than a dozen words to the stern-faced man who sat beside her driving the powerful car with a relaxed ease at a speed which would have dismayed her, if she hadn't lived on Crete long enough to know that many of the inhabitants regarded the ultra-low official speed limit as being dangerously slow.

Fortunately the thick, creamy ewe's milk yogurt supplied by room service the previous evening and liberally applied to her tender skin had wrought its vaunted magic, but she had used her mild sunburn as an excuse not to have dinner, retiring to her room after her shower, leaving Nik to his own devices.

Now, even the memory of their heated argument and Nik's confirmation of his previous intention of duping his father into believing Markos was his own flesh and blood could not detract from the mounting sense of excitement that was bringing her to a peak of expectation.

'We're entering Ierapetra now.' Nik spoke some time later as the wide main road approached the environs of the small town. 'The Villa Pasiphaë is about a kilometre the other side of the centre. Near enough to the source of things for easy access to the shops, tavernas and the safe town beach, but far enough away from the summer crowds for us to enjoy a deserted, wild shore which is still unspoiled even in the main season.'

'It's very attractive,' Karis voiced an honest opinion as the Mercedes left the main thoroughfare behind it.

'I think so,' Nik agreed pleasantly. 'The main industry is greenhouse culture—I expect you noticed the large polythene greenhouses as we entered the area. They supply cucumbers, tomatoes and melons to the rest of Europe.' He cast her a quick sideways glance. 'I imagine you already know that Ierapetra is the most southerly town in Europe and reputedly has the best weather of any place on Crete? When it's raining on the north coast the three mountain ridges down the centre of the island contain the bad weather and Ierapetra continues to enjoy sunshine. In fact, I believe it's the only place in Europe where bananas regularly fruit out of doors.'

'Really?' Karis murmured a polite interest. Certainly it was better to discuss the climate than to resurrect their differences of last night!

'Andriana loved this place.' Nik's voice was emotionless as he turned off the main highway on to a well-surfaced tree-lined road where Karis could see various detached properties scattered in what appeared a random fashion.

'And the climate seemed to agree with her. Although our main residence was just outside Athens, every year we spent the summer here . . . Markos enjoys it too, and it makes a pleasant break for my housekeeper Maria.'

Why did her heart clench every time he mentioned Andriana in those casual tones? After his crude announcement yesterday, she had no reason to weep for his tragedy. Better she kept her tears for herself! Yet it was an effort to mask the compassion she felt for him as her quick glance took in his rigidly held features.

Fortunately there was no need to comment as the car took a right turn, slowing down as the road surface beneath it deteriorated. Instead Karis caught her breath in spontaneous admiration as Nik applied the brakes, bringing the Mercedes to a stop and announcing briskly, 'Well, this is it, Karis. Welcome to the Villa Pasiphaë.'

'It's magnificent!' It was the gardens initially which brought forth Karis's spontaneous praise. They were lawned and terraced, planted with roses and geraniums which in the warmth of the early spring were already showing signs of life, with tubs of stark white lilies in full flower, their perfume assaulting her nostrils as she stepped from the car to inhale their scent, and she felt she might have been entering Paradise itself.

'I had it designed and laid by the firm who did the landscaping for the Supermare—one of the Christianides' Group hotels farther along the coast.' Nik sounded smug, as well he might. Even in the parched heat of summer Karis knew instinctively that the grounds of Pasiphaë would remain green and lush, their beauty hidden from the surrounding barren countryside by the copious trees which surrounded the boundaries, among which she recognised olives, lemons and the vibrant orange blossom of pomegranates.

Holding the wrought iron gate open for her, Nik indicated that she precede him up the stone steps leading to the front door. 'I'll garage the car in a moment,' he told her quietly. 'I imagine Markos is barely containing himself with excitement.'

'Nik . . .' Nausea assailed her as her legs seemed to turn to aspic and she grabbed his arm on which to support herself. 'Oh, Nik, what can I do . . . I think I'm going to faint.' He was the only person there to save her, and she turned to him, swaying, her blue eyes trying to focus on his face, as she read his concern.

'Take a deep breath . . .' One strong arm came round her shoulders, as she remembered how he had supported her at the London Acropolis after he had made his earth-shaking announcement. Only a few days ago—and it seemed a lifetime. 'It won't be such an ordeal—believe me!'

The door to the house opened before she could reply and Markos—because it could be no one else—hurled himself down the remaining steps to fling himself at Nik.

'Papa, Papa!' The childish face was alight with joy. 'Can I go to Chrisi on my name day? Maria says it's too early in the season and we might not be able to come back again, and we've got *calamari* for lunch because Tonia said I could choose and it had to be something special because you'd got married again and we were all going to be a happy once more like when Mama was with us . . .'

'Hush, *yiós mou*, hush!' Nik reproved gently, but the smile on his face was as joyous as the small boy's. 'One thing at a time, if you please. Maria is right when she worries about the weather—we shall have to wait and see what it's like first before I make promises, and I'm sure *calamari* are an excellent choice, because I know Karis enjoys them as much as you and I do.'

How could he possibly know that? Strength was returning to her limbs with every second as she obeyed Nik's injunction and drew the sweet-smelling air into her lungs. For a moment she was puzzled at his claim to knowledge of her appetite, then she remembered that day on the beach six years ago, when they had all lunched at a beach taverna on plates piled high with golden crispy fried squid dressed with lemon wedges, and she had declared her addiction for that specifically Mediterranean delicacy.

'. . . and yes, Karis and I are married, and I think you should say hello to her first, don't you? She's waited a long time to meet you, and we don't want her to think that you haven't any manners, do we?'

'Hallo, Karis—I'm Markos!' It was an artless smile he turned on her, so that her heart overflowed with tumultuous joy and relief. 'Maria said that you were the surprise Papa was bringing back from England with him but that I mustn't call you Mama unless you wanted me to. Do you want me to?'

'Oh, Markos!' She had never imagined their first meeting being like this—out in the open air, warmed by the sun, perfumed by the scent of lilies. Neither had she dared to hope for the open-hearted welcome her son would bestow on her. She'd been prepared to take things slowly, to keep her patience in the face of jealousy or opposition or even dislike. Now here was this beautiful child with his black curls and white-toothed grin asking if he could call her 'Mama'!

Without a second thought she stooped to gather him into her arms, holding him against her shoulder, as Nik's arm continued to support her, rejoicing in the sturdiness of bone and muscle as the warm young body settled against her own, suppressing the painful surge of emotion that threatened to choke her.

Once more she was holding the baby she had loved so dearly, the child created in a moment of compassion and affection while the dark threat of separation hung over herself and the young man who'd been the first person to cherish her since her father's desertion. Now Markos, the fruit of that union, as dark and attractive as his father had been, yet at the same time bearing an uncanny resemblance to the man who had reared him, had been restored to her. The years of heartbreak ended for ever as his warm cheek brushed against her own.

'I don't really mind what you call me.' Her arms tightened round the child in her arms as she shot an appealing look at Nik, who was regarding them both with a slight smile alleviating the harsh planes of his face. Receiving no help from that quarter, she made her own decision, taking into account how Nik himself and the other people who had known and loved Andriana would feel.

'Perhaps, sweetheart, to start with you should call me Karis, hmm? You see, "Mama" is a very special name and I don't think I deserve that yet. Perhaps when we've got to know each other a bit better and you're sure you like me . . .' She let the sentence trail into silence.

'OK,' Markos agreed easily. 'Maria says you're English. Will you teach me to speak English like Mama did? Papa says that all Greeks must learn English because the English aren't clever enough to learn Greek.' He frowned as Nik's unrestrained laughter echoed round the garden. 'But that can't be right, can it—because you speak Greek, and Mama spoke Greek too.'

'But Andriana—your mama *was* Greek . . .' Karis began.

This time it was Markos whose peals of childish laughter sounded in the warm afternoon air. 'Lots of people thought that, but she wasn't, was she, Papa?' He didn't wait for Nik's reply, continuing gravely, 'Mama was born in the USA. She was American!'

It just went to show how little she knew of Nik's background, Karis thought pensively as she carried her son into the villa, setting him down reluctantly once they had gained the cool marble interior of the house itself. Not that Andriana's nationality was important in itself, only

that all these years she had always thought of Nik's wife as
being traditionally Greek in culture and custom, taking a
back seat to the interests of her dynamic spouse.

Half an hour later, watching Nik in animated
conversation with Markos as the three of them lunched on
the wide terrace at the back of the house, overlooking a
large patio with a central swimming pool amidst tubs of
flowers and thick shrubs, Karis still found it difficult to
believe that Nik could have lived so happily with a North
American and still retained his aura of archetypal Greek
chauvinism.

Biting into the crisp, delicious fish that Maria had
served with a garnish of lemon, a dressing of seafood
sauce and a traditional Greek salad of tomatoes,
cucumber, and slivers of onion topped with a thick slice of
dry, pungent feta cheese, she supposed it must be that the
gentle and lovable Andriana had tamed her Greek lover,
turned him into the proverbial putty in her delicate
hands. Now, with her influence gone, Nik had returned
to the wild, become the heartless, feral predator that his
actions proclaimed him, yet, watching him with Markos,
it was difficult to believe this was the same man whose
tongue had lashed her so brutally the previous evening
and who had already given notice of his intention to break
the undertaking he had given her in London.

How would Andriana have reacted to her husband's
plot to deceive his father? she wondered. Would she, in
her place, have taken as firm a stand as she, Karis, had
taken, or would she have been pleased to see vengeance
taken against the man who had exhorted his son to obtain
a divorce on such cruel grounds?

'What is it, Karis?' Nik's softly voiced question
interrupted her sombre thoughts. 'Today's not a day for
sad memories or worries about the future. Whatever the
problems ahead, I guarantee you may enjoy today and

tonight without apprehension.'

'Oh!' She felt herself colouring as she translated his meaning. In all honesty, the sheer pleasure of holding Markos in her arms, and watching his vitality and obvious happiness, had temporarily removed all thoughts of the coming night from her mind. Now here was her husband reminding her of his intentions, but promising her a stay of execution so she could enjoy the first day of reunion with her son without concern for the immediate hours ahead.

'Markos wants to take you on a tour round the house when lunch is over, and then if you're not too tired he wants the three of us to go for a walk along the beach.' Nik didn't wait for her thanks for the armistice he had declared, knowing, perhaps, that they would have been grudgingly given.

'No, I'm not a bit tired,' she lied quickly, pushing to the back of her mind the restless hours she had spent the previous night as sleep eluded her. 'I'd love to see the beach. I don't know this part of the island at all, so I shall depend on you and Markos to help me find my way around!'

The beaming smile she received from her son was all the thanks she needed—enough to put new zest into her step as an hour later she left the villa with the two new men in her life.

'Thank you, Nik!' Impulsively she took his hand in her own at the end of the evening as the two of them left Markos's bedroom together after tucking him in for the night. 'I can't put what I feel into words—I should only burst into tears, but—but there's one thing I must say . . .'

'Yes?' His dark eyebrows lifted interrogatively.

'He's a lovely child—and it's all credit to you and Andriana. I'm so very, very grateful for everything you both did . . .' Despite a massive effort to control it her voice broke. 'And the chance you've given me to have him back . . . I'll do anything I can to prove it—except—except . . .' she faltered.

'Except lie to my father about his origin, eh?' His sombre eyes raked over her pleading face. 'Florina shouldn't have spoken to you as she did. Unfortunately she's an artiste and a very emotional one at that, who becomes drunk on the power of her own performance, and rarely thinks twice before she speaks on such occasions. It was perhaps only natural she should have assumed we were lovers and my father's wish to found a dynasty was about to be fulfilled. I take it that was the gist of what she implied?'

'Yes,' Karis nodded miserably. 'It seems he'd told her that unless you provided him with an acceptable heir, he'd marry again and produce his own—but of course you know that.'

'My father is a proud and stubborn man.' Reaching the bottom of the flight of stairs leading from the upstairs landing, Nik guided Karis to the pleasant living-room which ran along the back of the house, opening the door for her and continuing as she preceded him, 'He values the Christianides empire more than any living soul—man or woman. It's his one aim in life that the control of it stays in the family—which in his terms means his own flesh and blood.' Moving to a drinks cabinet against one wall, he paused. 'Will you join me in a Metaxa?'

'Please.' Watching his profile as he filled two brandy glasses, Karis saw the bitter tightness that thinned his mouth. Bringing one glass to her where she sat, Nik sprawled down on an easy chair opposite her, gazing down into the amber depths of the liquid before him.

'It was my grandfather and his brother who started the company after going to the USA. It was a struggle at first,

then they hit just the right note at the right time and went
public, keeping fifty-two per cent of the shares
themselves. After a while my grandfather came back to
Greece, married an Athenian and fathered Giorgios. On
their death, Giorgios inherited their shareholding, the
other twenty-six per cent being held by his uncle
Gregoris, who was still in the States.'

He turned the brandy glass in his strong lean hands,
warming it between his palms. 'But my father wasn't only
ambitious in those days, he was rash as well, and when he
saw an opportunity to expand into shipping he took it,
selling ten per cent of his shares to finance the venture,
certain that in a short time he would not only increase his
fortune considerably but also be able to buy back his
shares on the open market.'

He raised the glass to his lips, sipping at it thoughtfully.

Karis's eyes rested on his set face, gratified that he was
confiding some of his past history in her, yet uncertain
where the story was leading.

'And was he?' she prompted softly, leaning forward
and fixing her shining turquoise eyes on his dark gaze as
he set the glass down on the table before him.

'No.' The dark head shook. 'The shipping project
never really got off the ground, or should I say, into the
sea . . .' A humourless smile touched his mouth. 'So he
did the only other thing possible to regain his fortune. He
married for money.'

'You mean he and your mother . . .?' Karis stopped in
mid-sentence, seeing the pain reflected in the dark eyes
opposite her.

'Weren't in love with each other?' Nik gave a bitter
laugh. 'If only that had been true, instead of only half
true. Giorgios cared nothing for Irene, my mother, only
for the considerable dowry she brought with her . . . but
she . . .' He shook his head slowly from side to side. 'My

mother adored him; drawn like a moth to a candle, she wanted nothing more than to be loved and possessed by him. Unfortunately, after I was born and the line of inheritance assured, he treated her abominably, ignoring her for days on end, flaunting his mistresses in her face.'

Angrily he pushed himself to his feet, striding to the window and staring out into the darkness. 'Of course I was too young to realise what was going on at the time, but I did know she cried a lot and that she drank things that changed her from the loving, caring mother she could be to an hysterical, frightened woman who had little time for me.'

He paused again, and in the stretching silence Karis longed to go to him, to put her arm around him, sensing in the hard, virile outline of the man silhouetted against the window the sadness and bitterness of the youngster he had once been. Her own common sense restrained her. Nik was lost in a world of suffering to which she had no right of entry. She heard the racking sigh that left his body, then his quiet voice continued.

'I was twelve years old when she died. At the time the verdict was accidental death—she'd been taken ill and choked to death alone in her room. Years later I discovered that her illness had been brought about by a handful of sleeping tablets followed by half a bottle of brandy.'

'Nik—I'm so sorry . . .' The urge to go to him and take him in her arms was doubly strong now as he turned and Karis saw the twisted lines of his tortured face. He had always seemed so composed, so much in charge of his own destiny. How could she have guessed at the traumatic childhood he must have suffered?

'Are you?' He took a long shuddering breath. 'Yes, it was tough at the time. Later—well, I came to terms with it. My father's behaviour, after all, hadn't been that different from many of his business colleagues; it was just unfortunate that my mother loved him so desperately and wanted him exclusively to herself. She had all the material possessions she could have desired; many women would have been satisfied . . .'

I wouldn't have been . . . Karis bit her tongue to stop the words from leaving her mouth. Why had Nik revealed so much of his early life to her? she wondered. Probably to show her why he felt himself entitled to Giorgios's fortune—hadn't a good part of it been provided by his own mother? Yet he already owned twenty-six per cent of the shares, she pondered, remembering Florina's words. Presumably he had inherited those directly from his grandfather's brother's side of the family.

'Nik——' She rose to her feet, moving towards him to lay a gentle arm on his sleeve, feeling the muscle of his arm contract beneath her touch. 'Thank you for telling me. I—I can understand better how you must feel . . .'

'Can you?' He looked down at her and the torment on his face shocked her. Instinctively her hand tightened on his arm as she sought the words to comfort him. Then she saw his jaw tighten, and knew he was deliberately raising a shield against his pity. 'I doubt that very much, *yineka mou.*'

Pain registering in the deep peacock blue of her eyes, Karis winced at the ironic way he had referred to her as his wife. First his mother, then Andriana . . . How had she had the temerity to claim a knowledge of what he had suffered? That had to be what he was thinking. But she wasn't really without understanding—not after the years of being deprived of Markos.

Even now, though her heart was overflowing with the joy of their reunion, she knew she had lost for ever the magic days of his babyhood, those first vital steps of crawling, walking, teething, speaking . . .

Now Nik had made it clear that he would stop at nothing to ensure his inheritance, and she was being offered what she had never dared to contemplate since Markos's adoption—the joy of bearing a child and watching him grow up. The child of a man who didn't love her, didn't even like her, but into whose path fate had thrown her not once, but twice!

The thought of sharing with Nik the intimate relationship necessary for such a possibility should have seemed as unattractive as it had done a few days ago in London. Quite suddenly it didn't. A warm glow of yearning thrust through her body. Nik's baby—as strong and beautiful as her darling Markos—the most wondrous gift a woman could give the man she loved. She had never been able to see Yanís's face on the birth of his baby son. It was a pleasure Nik too had been denied. Something she could give him. In that brief instant, while her face glowed and her eyes sparkled unknowingly, she saw in her mind's eye the look of wonder on her husband's face as she handed to him for the first time the shawl-wrapped parcel which was his child—their child . . .

With a small cry of horror at the way her thoughts had betrayed her, Karis stepped away from the silent man whose dark eyes seemed to be penetrating into her deepest soul. This strange agitation which was sending shivers of delight through every cell of her body, firing her nerves into unwarranted disturbance, causing her pulse to beat with an alarming rapidity—it had to be maternal longing, didn't it? It couldn't possibly be that, against all logical understanding, she was beginning to love the man she had married?

'Don't be alarmed, Karis.' His face was tautly controlled as his gaze flickered over her dazed face. 'My first concern for the next few days is to see you and Markos forge the relationship which should already be yours. When the time comes for us to do something about making my father a happy man—be sure I'll let you know.' He smiled grimly and there was no amusement in the depths of his sombre eyes. 'And now perhaps you'd like to watch a little television while you finish your brandy.'

It was a pleasant enough way to spend the evening, but Karis remembered nothing of the pictures that flashed before her eyes, all her awareness concentrated on the man seated silently across the room from her. To live with Nik *not* loving him was something she had been prepared to accept—but to live with him *loving* him—when she could expect nothing in return—that was going to be monstrous!

Later that evening, she went alone to the double room which Maria had prepared for them. Admiring the light, polished wood floor and the cream and apricot décor of her surroundings, she undressed quickly after her shower, donning a pale green full-length silk nightdress with a simple opera top, and climbed in between the sweet-smelling bleached cotton sheets, glad to discover a thick fluffy apricot-coloured blanket beneath the heavy cream quilt. At this time of the year the nights could be cold, especially, she supposed, in a double bed when there was to be no contact between the occupants.

She must have been sleeping when Nik joined her, for she had no recollection of his coming to share the bed. Some time in the small hours of the morning she awakened, conscious of the presence beside her, aware of his slow almost silent breathing.

Curiosity getting the better of her, she raised herself on one elbow to gaze down at his sleeping face, illuminated by the moon's thin blue light as it filtered in through the half-closed shutters. There was an untypical vulnerability now about the carved lines of his Saracen features, an unexpected softness that tugged at her heart. Dear lord, in following her own selfish desires hadn't she done this man a dreadful disservice, despite the fact that it had been at his demand?

Suddenly it was as if a curtain had lifted, revealing the truth. She had watched him with her child, seen his tenderness, the gentleness and love in the firm hands that had touched Markos. Nik Christianides wasn't the cold, hard man she had always thought him. Misguided maybe, in attempting to fool his father, but everything she had learned about him these last few days pointed to his being a man of passion, capable of an abiding and deep love for the right woman. Only that woman had been Andriana, and if it were possible for another woman to replace her in his life, then he had made it plain it was definitely not herself.

Tentatively, so as not to disturb him, she reached out a hand, stroking the dark hair from his forehead with gentle fingers. Whatever joy she would bring to Markos—and however mixed Nik's motives had been in asking her to marry him, she no longer doubted they had been chiefly in Markos's interest—there could only ever be unfulfilment between herself and the man beside her.

'We should never have married,' she whispered in an agony of self-reproach. 'Oh, Nik . . . what have we done?'

CHAPTER NINE

A SHARP tap at the door awakened Karis the following morning. Pushing herself up in the wide bed, registering the fact that Nik was no longer beside her, she called out, 'Come in,' changing it to *'Embrós, parakalo'*, as she remembered where she was.

'Kyrios Nikolaos thought you would like breakfast in bed.' Maria entered bearing a tray which she set down on the bedside table.

'Oh, you shouldn't have troubled,' Karis smiled at the woman's dour face. 'I could easily have joined the others, but thank you all the same.'

'It's no trouble. Kyria Andriana always had a tray in the morning.'

'Yes, I see.' Karis felt rebuked, especially as she received no answering smile. Neither did she want to point out that Andriana had unfortunately lacked her own strength and health. Clearly Maria still mourned Nik's first wife and held a not incomprehensible resentment of her successor. She had suspected it yesterday when Nik had introduced them. The older woman's attitude had been courteous but cold. Ah, well, she consoled herself, it was only to be expected. Perhaps in time Maria would grow to tolerate her, especially if she were able to endear herself to Markos, and made no attempt to interfere with the way Maria ran the household.

'Well, it's lovely to be spoiled,' she contented herself with saying, 'but I mustn't make a habit of it. Maria, do you know where my—my husband is at the moment? I was still asleep when he got up.'

'He and the child are having breakfast together.' For the first time the expression of the older woman's eyes softened. 'Markos was so excited because it's his name-day that he was up at six this morning to open his presents.'

Of course! Karis's hand rose to her mouth as she watched Maria leave the room. April the twenty-fifth—St Mark's Day! Markos had said something about it to Nik at their first meeting: only, used as she was, to birthday celebrations instead of name-days, it had temporarily escaped her memory.

All wasn't lost, though! Scrambling out of bed, she unearthed one of her suitcases and drew from its already diminished depths four gift-wrapped parcels. She had bought them in London before leaving, but, not wanting to appear to buy her son's favour, she had deliberately refrained from producing them yesterday. Now she had a reason!

Not that they were particularly special or expensive, she thought with a wry smile as she returned to bed, taking the gifts with her and turning her attention to the neatly arranged tray at her side from which the heady aroma of freshly brewed coffee assailed her. Having guessed Markos wouldn't lack much, she had deliberately sought to include something different to interest him—a beautifully designed double-decker London bus; a glove puppet of a Yeoman Warder; a model of Concorde and a box of Lego bricks. She hoped, desperately, that his appetite wouldn't be too jaded by Nik's largesse not to find some enjoyment out of at least one of the items!

She had just finished her second cup of coffee and guiltily eaten the last croissant when a softer tap at the door alerted her.

'*Embrós, parakalo!*' she called out, the sudden surge of her pulse rate justified as Markos came in, a mischievous grin on his face.

'Papa said I mustn't disturb you if you didn't want to see me yet,' he announced, coming to stand by the bed and gazing up at her.

'Of course I want to see you, darling.' Impulsively she reached out and lifted him on to the bed, giving him a quick warm cuddle, overjoyed when he accepted her embrace without any sign of awkwardness. 'I was hoping you'd come in to see me—I just couldn't wait to wish you *hronia pola* and give you the presents I brought for you from England!'

'Can I open them now?' His small face beamed with pleasure as his dark eyes dwelt on the assortment of parcels.

'Of course,' Karis nodded, praying he wouldn't be disappointed.

From his cries of delight as he ripped the paper away one would have thought he'd never had a gift in his life before.

'*Efcharisto poli, efcharisto poli,* Karis . . .' The guttural expression of thanks died in his throat as he threw his arms round her and buried his face against the warm silk of her nightdress. 'This is going to be the best name-day I ever had!' he announced proudly. 'Papa says he's checked up on the weather and Crete is having a mini heatwave, so we can have a picnic on Chrisi, and he's going to let me invite some of my other friends and Tonia can come too!'

'That sounds lovely,' Karis enthused, catching a glimpse of the morning sun probing its way through the half-shut blinds. 'I guess I'd better get up and get myself ready.'

'Can you play with me first?' The artless question took her by surprise.

'Well, I guess so, darling—if it isn't a very long game.'

'No, no, it's not. It's called The Three Billygoats Gruff.'

Karis wrinkled her brow, memories of her childhood stirring at the back of her mind. 'Something to do with three goats and a troll guarding a bridge, isn't it?' she asked.

'Yes!' Markos clapped his hands together, delighted at her knowledge. '*You* have to be the naughty troll in charge of the bridge, and *I'm* the three billygoats Gruff and I have to cross over. The little goat and the next biggest are frightened and turn back, but the biggest one knocks the troll off the bridge and they can all go over and eat the grass on the other side.'

'Mm, I remember it,' Karis smiled wryly. It wasn't the ideal way to start the morning, but nothing would make her say so!

'I'm a troll, fol-de-rol . . .' Two goats already repulsed from clambering across the bed, Karis was now in full throat, rising to her knees to confront her son as he took on the role of the largest, most fierce billygoat. 'You can't cross my bridge!'

'Yes, I can!' Markos was shouting in his excitement. 'I'm the biggest, toughest billygoat and I'm going to throw you off!'

Together they wrestled, Karis marvelling in the strength of the small body which tested its strength against her own. Of course he had to win. Even if it hadn't been in the story she would have let him, but he was enjoying fighting for victory and she was going to let him have the triumph of a hard-won battle.

'Oh—oh——!' She'd started to slip for real, thrust out an arm to steady herself before landing on the polished wood floor, and caught the edge of the tray. There was a clatter of falling metal and china and a thud as she landed ignominiously among the debris.

'I won! I won!' The springs of the bed danced as an elated Markos claimed his bridge for his brother goats.

There was a sound of running footsteps, the door burst open and Nik entered the room to gaze at the scene in astonishment.

'Panaghia mou!' A dull flush of colour darkened his cheekbones as his eyes went from the excited child on the bed to Karis, who was still trying to get her breath back from her

harder-than-expected tumble. 'What the hell's going on here?'

'I won, Papa! I pushed Karis out of bed!'

'Nik, please!' Quickly she interrupted as Nik's eyes darkened with anger and turned their full glare on her son. 'Please don't be cross. We were only playing, and I guess we got a bit over-enthusiastic.' Turquoise eyes clouded with concern sought his gaze beseechingly. 'I'm dreadfully sorry about the breakages, but it really was all my fault. My hand caught the tray—I just didn't think to move it.' Please don't spoil it for us, she begged silently. Just when everything was going so well—oh, please, Nik, don't spoil it today of all days.

'There's nothing that can't be replaced.' He dismissed the mess on the floor with a shrug of his broad shoulders, but his face remained stern. 'But what about you? Are you hurt, Karis?' He offered her his hand and drew her to her feet, suddenly aware as she followed the direction of Nik's gaze that the fragile silk of her nightdress was doing very little to conceal the rounded swell of her pale breasts.

'I'm fine!' It wasn't strictly true, because she'd have a few bruises the next day, but nothing would have provoked her to say so.

'I'm sorry, Karis . . .' Markos's face was woebegone. 'I thought you were just playing.'

'I was, darling,' she reassured him quickly. 'Honestly, there's nothing wrong with me!'

'It seems a little early for bedroom games.' Nik's face was expressionless as he addressed them both, and if there was any double meaning intended for her, he never betrayed it with even a flicker of an eyelid. 'And I suggest that next time you feel inclined to wrestle each other you're both a little less boisterous!'

'Yes, Papa.' Markos clambered down from the bed as Nik crouched down to pick up the scattered pieces of crockery, placing them on the tray before rising to his feet.

Pausing on the threshold, he ushered Markos from the room, before turning to address Karis once more.

'I've promised Markos we'll take a boat over to Chrisi this morning and have a picnic lunch there. It's just a deserted sand atoll with a few windswept trees and scrub, but arguably one of the best beaches in Greece, if not the world.' A small gleam of amusement glowed in his sable eyes. 'From what I remember of you, I think you'll enjoy it.'

This time she'd make sure she didn't burn! Having applied suncream to all her exposed parts, Karis dressed in a pretty cotton sundress over a light bra and briefs, deciding to take a woollen cardigan with her for the journey across to the island. It was too early in the season to take chances.

They arrived on the isle of Chrisi about an hour and a half after leaving the little harbour of Ierapetra in a small motor cruiser Nik had hired specially for the trip since it was out of season and the tourist motor launches weren't operating. Markos had chosen three small friends to accompany him, all male, Karis noted with unexpressed amusement at the immature male's prediliction for companions of his own sex, and they had collected Tonia, an attractive, pleasant twenty-year-old enjoying the last days of her Easter holiday, from her house in the village.

Rather concerned when the boat had entered an area of mist some time after leaving the mainland, and only partially reassured by Nik's telling her it wasn't an unusual phenomenon and would disperse before they reached their destination, Karis was enthralled when, true to his prediction, they emerged the other side into a cloudless sky and cerulean blue seas so clear that it was possible to see the rocks on the sandy bottom.

'We'll moor here and walk across to the other side where the main beach is,' Nik told her. Dressed in brief denim shorts, a white cotton T-shirt stretched across his wide shoulders, a pair of espadrilles on his feet, his exposed legs muscled and tanned, he looked like a publicity photograph for a Greek holiday, Karis thought whimsically as, having switched off the engine and allowed the boat to drift towards the shore, he jumped lithely overboard, securing the vessel with a thick rope to an iron stanchion cemented into an outcrop of rocks.

As the children ran towards a narrow path leading through the low scrub at the back of the beach, followed by Tonia, Karis handed the picnic hamper packed by Maria over the side to Nik, before turning to gather up the large beach-bag full of towels and suntan lotions. Expecting to hand this over to him as well as he returned, she was surprised when he held out his arms to her.

'Put your arms round my neck and I'll lift you and the beach-bag down together,' he grinned up at her.

Karis hesitated, knowing she could have jumped down as easily as he had—it would have hardly mattered if her dress had got a bit splashed. But one look at those beautifully muscled arms, the slightly impatient yet mocking expression on his face, and suddenly the idea of being held against him for a few seconds seemed eminently desirable. Besides, she wasn't one of those discourteous females who insisted on equality at the price of good manners.

'Thank you, Nik,' she murmured, entrusting herself to his strong arms with utter confidence.

'There!' For a moment her whole body glowed as she felt his chest hard beneath the soft shirt, against her soft breasts, half crushing them as he hoisted her upwards, held her against himself for a split second, then taking a few strides lowered her gently to the beach. 'Let's follow the others.'

Her heart pounding at the brief proximity she had shared with her husband, Karis drew a deep breath, unnerved by the irrational way her senses were responding, as she allowed Nik to lead the way.

Chrisi was magic. Karis had known it intuitively from that first moment when its low shape had emerged, sungirt, from the mists, but even then she wasn't prepared for the almost unearthly beauty of the magnificent stretch of silver sand which greeted her eyes as she reached the highest part of the scrubland and saw it at her feet.

'Impressive, eh?' Nik watched her as she shaded her eyes. 'Wait until you actually tread on it!'

A few minutes later she was doing just that, her sandal-shod feet crunching on millions of tiny rainbow-coloured shells, each one no more than a millimetre in diameter, as the path through the scrub gave way to the extreme end of the sweeping bay. Tonia and the children were already walking away from them by the water's edge, but Karis paused, staring at the ground.

'I've never seen anything like it!' She crouched down, lifting handfuls of the tiny crustaceans and letting them trickle through her fingers. However deeply she dug there seemed no end to them—blue, bronze, white, purple, each one seemingly different from the next, each perfectly formed. 'How did they get here? I mean, the main beach we went to yesterday had very few shells on it.'

Nik shrugged. 'Who knows? Currents, maybe. In a few hundred years they may all have gone, worn down by the winter storms into as fine a shell beach as the rest of the bay.'

'This is an incredible place . . .' Karis's hair lifted in the slight breeze, tendrils blowing across her forehead as she turned to face the sea, seeing its slow suck against vast tabletop-smooth rocks, between which pools of water swirled and eddied. 'Can we look at the pools?' As excited as a child, Karis had already started moving before Nik's lazy tones gave consent.

'We can do what we like, *agapi mou*.' The easy endearment fell easily from Nik's lips, a sign perhaps that he too found this place relaxing. 'The island's ours for the next few hours—no other boats, no other people. During the summer there's an excellent bar/restaurant, but even that's not open today.' He followed her to the rocks, waiting patiently while she scanned their shallow depths, delighting in watching the tiny transparent fishes flitting across their surfaces, discernible only by the shadows they cast on the sandy bottom.

'Here . . .' He stooped suddenly to pick something up, offering it to her for her inspection.

'What is it?' Intrigued, Karis took from his hand what appeared to be a largish shell half immersed in a thick deposit. 'It looks as if it's covered in cement. Has someone been building here?'

Nik shook his head. 'It's volcanic lava, what the experts call "tuf". It's possible that the ancient Minoan civilisation of Crete was destroyed by some kind of volcanic eruption and the ashes fell here. Some people even believe that the island of Santorini is all that is left of the ancient civilisation of Atlantis, and that when Atlantis disintegrated the effects were felt as far away as here.'

'You mean this shell could have been around for a couple of thousand years?' Karis stared at it, achingly aware how short human life was in comparison with the evidence of previous cultures so much in abundance in the Eastern Mediterranean.

'Makes our own problems seem a little insignificant in comparison, doesn't it?' He had picked up her own mood, as, eyes narrowed against the sun, he took the shell from her unresisting hand and returned it to the beach. 'Come, we'd better give Tonia a hand—although she seems to be in her element!'

An hour later, sitting on a towel on the sand, Karis couldn't but agree with Nik's conclusion. The young Greek girl was full of life and energy, organising the boys into ball games and races, paddling with them in the sea, and generally leaving Karis herself and Nik to enjoy the brilliance of the day undisturbed.

It was a pity, Karis opined to herself, that she hadn't put on a swimsuit. Somehow she hadn't expected the sun to be so blazing or the sea so warm at this time of year. Now the clear, shallow aquamarine water beckoned her and she felt an aching disappointment that she couldn't accept its invitation.

'How about a walk along the beach?' Nik interrupted her thoughts, rising to his feet and offering her his hand, pre-empting a refusal if she'd intended to make one. 'The kids'll be fine here with Tonia.'

'Of course they will!' Tonia, long since having shed her shorts and top to appear in a sleek one-piece costume, was busy organising rides on an inflatable mattress. 'They'll be quite safe—the sea's shallow for a long way out and there's hardly a ripple on it.'

'We'll be back in an hour for lunch, then.' Nik's smile encompassed the children and their playmate, as, having pulled Karis to her feet, he reached for the beachbag and took out a couple of towels.

'Surely we won't be gone that long?' Karis demured.

'Why not?' An arm curled round her waist, so she was obliged to go with him. 'Isn't it the most natural thing in the world for lovers to want to be alone for a few moments in a paradise like this?'

'But we're not lovers . . .' she started to protest, and heard Nik's low laugh.

'Not yet, Karis *mou*. That is a pleasure that still awaits us, but my reputation would suffer badly should Tonia guess it.'

Not certain whether he was laughing at her or not, Karis held her tongue. Nik at the moment was as relaxed and casual as she had ever seen him, softened by what she could only term as the magic of Chrisi. For the time being a truce existed between them and she might as well enjoy it. Try to forget that a part of him was irretrievably lost to her, buried in the past with the lovely, ill-fated Andriana.

'Are you happy, Karis?'

They had been walking in silence for several minutes and the question took her by surprise.

'Of course.' She met Nik's questioning gaze, conscious of the heavy thud of her heart. 'I can't really believe what's happened, though. It's like a dream!' She gave a nervous laugh. 'I still feel I shall wake up one morning and it will all be gone—Markos, the villa, this incredibly beautiful island—everything!'

'Even me?' Nik stopped walking and swung her round to face him, fastening her startled eyes with a predator's intense stare, his voice oddly cool. 'You didn't mention me, Karis. Could that be because I'm the serpent in your newly discovered Eden?'

'Nik, you're hurting me!' she protested as his fingers pressed against her arm with a latent cruelty. 'I didn't mean that at all!' The simple reason was that she hadn't mentioned him because she hadn't wanted to betray her growing need of his companionship.

'It's a part of the bargain, my beauty . . .' He stared into her eyes. 'Markos and I come as a joint package. You'll never take him away from me!'

'I wouldn't want to!' The harshness on his lean face aroused an answering ache inside her. 'Do you really think I'm not grateful for what you and Andriana did for him? That I've stopped thanking God for your charity since the moment I found out you'd adopted him?' She was trembling both with the intensity of her own feelings and as a result of the piercing threatening blackness of Nik's unremitting gaze.

'I don't want your gratitude!' He hurled the words at her so that she flinched at his vehemence. 'All I want is your co-operation in ensuring that he has a happy family life without trial or trauma!'

'And a brother or sister to ensure you don't lose control of the Christianides empire!' she flung back. She saw his mouth tighten ominously and cursed herself for not holding her tongue as she felt the strength and violence of his anger at her tart response flow over her.

For a few seconds she closed her eyes, blotting out the picture of his anger.

'Look at me, Karis.' His low voice was softly controlled, the command accompanied by a slight shake, so that her eyes flew open in automatic response. 'Florina gave you a good reason why I should have a child of my own. Am I to understand that your gratitude, so freely expressed a second ago, has limitations to it?'

'No . . .' Karis swallowed resolutely. 'I have no intention of refusing your reasonable demands.'

'Oh, Karis!' Nik released her arms, lifting one hand to stroke the side of her flushed cheek, as his voice softened to a husky murmur. 'You stand there looking at me with those incredible eyes, and talk to me of reason. Who is to be the judge of what is reasonable or not?'

How could she answer such a question? The very thought of Nik taking her body without love or respect made her shrink invisibly, neutralising the surge of awareness she felt at his touch.

'No answer?' He took pity on her. 'Well, it's early days yet. Perhaps when you've settled down you won't find the prospect of being my wife so distasteful. Now, how about a swim?'

'I can't.' Relieved that the subject was ended, she would have liked nothing better than to cool her burning flesh in the limpid waters, and her disappointment echoed in her voice. 'I didn't bring a swimsuit with me.'

'So what?' Airily Nik dismissed her excuse. 'It's hardly a crowded beach, is it? Even Tonia and the children who are the only other occupants are several hundred yards away, discernible only as moving black dots. You're hardly going to shock anyone if you go in without one.'

'In my undies, you mean?' She'd already thought of that and dismissed it as impracticable. 'They'd take too long to dry and I couldn't put my dress on again without them—the material's far too thin.'

'Then go in naked,' Nik suggested indifferently. Not waiting to see her shocked reaction, he crossed his arms, grabbing his own T-shirt by its bottom and dragging it upwards. It was a typically male action of undressing, with none of the finesse a woman used in removing clothes.

Transfixed, Karis watched as the shirt stretched momentarily from elbow to elbow, revealing the powerful swell of well-developed triceps, a broad expanse of tanned chest, the skin taut over a sturdy yet graceful ribcage. Despite herself her eyes followed the vertical line that cleaved a passage between the ridged muscles of his torso from chest to neat navel and dwelt for a tremulous moment on the hard flat plane of his abdomen girdled by the band of his hipster shorts.

Unwillingly an old memory reasserted itself. That day six years ago when Nik had joined Elizabeth and her and the children on the beach. He had been married and she had been in love with Yanís, but something had sparked between them, that odd electric tension that had left her feeling ill at ease. Nothing had changed. He was still able to curdle her emotions, arouse an unwilling response just by being there. Her breath caught in her throat as, having discarded his shirt, he divested himself of his shorts, revealing a narrow band of bathing slip which clung to his hollowed loins.

Fascinated, Karis found she couldn't tear her gaze away from him as, back turned to her, he paused to stretch, revelling in the feel of the breeze on his skin, the heat of the sun on his near-naked body, his fingers combing through his thick hair.

How deceptive was his apparent litheness, she accorded to herself, suppressing a little shiver, knowing that beneath that golden, silken skin powerful muscles lay at rest. Whatever Nik Christianides wanted he would have—be it success, money or a child of his own. Perhaps in time he would even find someone to love as much as he had loved Andriana. After all, he had made it perfectly clear to her that he reserved the right to have relationships out of marriage!

Her eyes remained on him as he covered the short distance to the sea, envying him as he plunged into its welcoming embrace. Damn her own stupidity for not putting a swimsuit on under her dress! She felt hot and sticky and mentally disrupted by the words that had passed so unexpectedly between them. Who would have guessed Nik's reasonable manner would disappear so quickly, the short armistice broken by that quick cross-fire? Her mind longed as much as her body for the solace of cool water, as a surge of defiance challenged her regular sense of propriety.

Why shouldn't she do as Nik had suggested and swim in the nude? Adam and Eve in the Garden of Eden could hardly have been afforded more privacy! A reluctant smile turned her mouth. It was hardly the ideal analogy if one believed their nudity had been a major element in their downfall! But the water was tempting and she needn't stay in very long, taking only a little dip, returning to re-clothe herself long before Nik returned to the shore.

There was no sign of Nik as she made her decision, loosening the straps of her sundress and letting it fall to the sand before undoing the clasp of her bra and quickly removing her briefs.

The sea struck her as cold as her heated body entered. Conscious of her nudity, she plunged forward without letting her skin acclimatise, submerging herself with bated breath. The first shock of immersion over, she soon found she was enjoying herself. How different the sensation was from wearing a swimsuit or even a bikini! She was astonished at the erotic sensation of the water swirling through her limbs, the marvellous sense of freedom, the feeling of being at one with nature. Just out of her depth, she swam and tumbled and floated, dulling her mind to everything but the sensual experience she was undergoing.

'Karis!' Nik's voice pierced her lethargy as she hurriedly trod water. Too late now to get dressed before he saw her. He was standing on the beach, holding her towel over his arm and beckoning to her. 'Time for lunch!'

Hell! This was the last thing she'd wanted to happen.

'OK,' she called back, making no move to swim nearer. 'You go back and I'll follow.'

She received no answer. Nik merely unfolded the towel and held it out towards her, inviting her to take advantage of its comfort.

What to do? She'd been in much longer than she had intended, could already feel goosepimples on her legs, and Nik was standing as resolute as a Colossus, knowing and enjoying her predicament.

'Come along, *agapi*. We can't keep the others waiting.' He spoke to her as if she were nothing but a difficult child, and suddenly she knew it was stupid to be embarrassed. Nik was her husband, had every intention of becoming her lover, and she certainly wasn't the first woman he'd ever seen without her clothes on. She was damned if she'd let him embarrass her!

'Coming!' she called sweetly, and began her slow graceful progress towards him, wading through the water, making no attempt to hide herself from his avid gaze as portion by portion her sun-flushed skin was revealed.

It wasn't easy, but she managed it, dissociating her actions from the reality, imagining she was an actress playing a part.

Only when she was within feet of him did she wonder with a sinking heart if Nik would tease her by moving backwards from her, taking with him the towel which would give her back her modesty, thus prolonging her ordeal. But he stayed rooted to the spot, his eyes narrowed against the sun, their glittering pupils fixed on her, as head held high, she came within reach of him.

She was shivering as he wrapped the towel around her beneath her shoulders, tucking in the ends to make a sarong, before patting her covered skin gently to absorb the moisture.

'Karis?' The way he said her name made the blood thrum in her ears. When he whispered it again, still in the same husky voice, she stared at him in mute enquiry.

Gently he drew her closer, his hands massaging her towel-covered back. She could feel the powerful beating of his heart and hear the heavy rasping sound of his breath, and when his grip tightened on her and he held her hard against his own body she accepted his arousal as her due, caught as both of them were in the spell of the island. As an answering response seared through her she lifted her mouth to his, shivering again as she tasted the cool saltiness of his kiss.

'You can still make me want you, Karis *mou* . . .' His mouth moved possessively over her face, as his hands went to support her head, turning her slightly so that when he took her mouth again he was overpoweringly dominant. 'How long do you think I can go on like this—living in the same house, sleeping in the same bed without touching you—now that we're agreed that you will bear my children?'

It must have been a rhetorical question, because he didn't release her mouth long enough for her to answer and she was drowning in kisses more dangerous than the threat of any ocean. Her hands found his shoulders, her fingers explored the powerful deltoid muscles of his back before lifting to tangle in the sweet, sticky saltiness of his ebony hair.

Of course he didn't love her, she knew that. He was reacting like any other virile man who hadn't made love to a woman for some time and who was confronted with a naked female walking from the sea like some dream fantasy, but locked in his arms she could force herself to forget that—remembering only that he was her husband and she had every right to enjoy his caresses.

Nik was shaking when he released her. She could feel the tremors quivering through his body as he pushed her away from him.

'You were always the temptress.' Sloe-black eyes seemed to accuse her for his own lack of self-control. 'I'm going in for another quick swim. Get dressed and on your way—I'll catch you up.'

He turned, running into the calm water, throwing himself forward as soon as it was deep enough and striking out with a powerful freestyle.

It was late afternoon when they left the island after sitting in the shade of the sun umbrellas they had brought with them, enjoying the ample food and wine Maria had provided. No one spoke much on the return journey, the children healthily tired by their activities, Nik deep in his own thoughts and Tonia apparently content to relax after her own hectic day.

Everyone had outstanding days in their life, twenty-four hours they would gladly relive, Karis supposed. The day she had held Markos in her arms again had been one such day for her. Today would be another, and not least of all because of those few moments of fantasy she had enjoyed as Nik's mouth had claimed her own with an aching hunger.

Markos's friends delivered back to their families, Tonia bidden a fond and grateful farewell, Nik carried his adopted son back into the Villa Pasiphaë, as Karis followed closely behind them.

'Kyrios Nikolaos . . .' Maria rushed out of the kitchen to

meet them. 'Thank heaven you're back! Thespinis Nikoletta has been on the phone. You're needed urgently in Athens. She's already booked a seat for you on a charter flight leaving in two hours' time!'

CHAPTER TEN

'I PHONED Nikoletta's apartment, but there's no answer.' Nik, showered, shaved and dressed in a lightweight fawn suit, zipped up a smart leather travelling bag with an impatient flourish, as Karis watched, a premonition of impending disaster having ruined her previous sense of well-being. 'Apparently all she said to Maria was that Giorgios had been detained somewhere and wanted me to take his place at the special board meeting later this evening.'

'Do you know what the meeting's about?' Karis hazarded as he checked the time on his wristwatch.

'Yes, that won't be a problem. It's concerning the costs of a new development in Rhodes. My father had my proxy vote, so with neither of us there the whole meeting would have been a fiasco. He would have known that I'd step into his place, but it's damned annoying all the same!'

Was it? Karis wondered. Oh, certainly Nik wouldn't appreciate being taken for granted or having his plans disrupted so arbitrarily, but wouldn't it give him the opportunity of seeing Nikoletta again? A surge of pure jealousy made her heart ache. The man she had married was all male, capable of great self-control, undoubtedly, but earlier on the beach she had been left in no doubt of his sensual nature. If she were honest, she admitted to herself, part of her happiness on the return journey from the island had been because she had held this taunting, fragile hope that Nik might have begun to care for her enough to put aside his reservations as to her past, and to have actually begun to accept that she hadn't been the mindless promiscuous flirt he had previously labelled her.

Now he was on his way to Athens—and Nikoletta; the woman his father had wanted him to marry. How did the Greek woman fit into the picture? Why should *she* be deputed to pass on Giorgios's message anyway? As far as Karis knew, Nikoletta had no connection with the Christianides business. Was it perhaps some plot the two of them had hatched to drag Nik away from her?

No. She was being psychotic. Nik wasn't a man to be manipulated against his will—besides, Nik's father had appeared to accept her . . .

'How long will you be gone?' she asked, making a determined effort to banish her own fears as Nik lifted his bag.

'As short a time as possible,' he said tersely. 'As soon as I find out what's going on I'll be in touch with you—probably tomorrow, so don't wait up tonight. Where's Markos?'

'Having something to eat in the kitchen with Maria.' She followed him down the open-tread staircase into the square entrance hall. 'He's going to be very disappointed that you're leaving.'

'He has you,' Nik told her curtly. 'Now you can see why I was so anxious to marry again. This isn't the first time I've had to leave home at a moment's notice.' His mouth twisted in a rueful grimace. 'At least this time it's not for the other side of the world!'

'I'm glad your decision has been justified so soon before you had cause to regret it!' Karis spoke tartly, knowing it was childish to taunt him, but the bald statement of her role had stung her vulnerable spirit. Making a move to walk past him, she found herself stopped in her tracks as Nik swung round to confront her.

'Am I going to have cause to regret it, Karis *mou*?' He asked the question softly, but there was a dangerous light behind his dark eyes that warned her she should be careful how she answered.

'Who knows?' she shrugged lightly. 'I haven't had much practice at being a wife and mother. I might not come up to your expectations.'

'But you love Markos!' Suddenly she found her chin imprisoned by the span of his fingers as he forced her face upwards, making it impossible to avoid the intensity of his scrutiny. 'If I hadn't already been convinced of it when I spoke to you in London, after seeing you together, I would have no doubt of it.' She couldn't speak, wouldn't have even if his firm grasp had allowed her to move her jaw, but the message in her eyes was unmistakable. With a brief laugh, Nik released her face.

'So you see, you already fulfil the first requirement necessary in my wife. As for the others, what were the adjectives you yourself used in London?' His dark gaze taunted her as he supplied his own answer. 'Beauty, obedience, intelligence, domesticity . . .' His head tilted sideways, his eyes perceptively sweeping over her. 'Beauty you certainly have—as any man seeing you rise like Venus from the foam would testify; intelligence, undoubtedly . . . as for domesticity and obedience, the first is unimportant since I can buy domestic efficiency, and the last . . .' He paused to trace the shape of her mouth with one slow finger. 'The last I believe you will give me in your own interests, né?'

'I've already told you I wouldn't refuse any reasonable request.' It was the most she was prepared to admit, and the words came stiffly from her mouth. Nik at his autocratic worst made her hackles rise, stirring a primeval desire to oppose him, fight him . . . even though the outcome would be inevitable and to her detriment. Always at the back of her mind was the knowledge that Markos didn't know who she was. Until Nik was prepared to tell his adopted son the truth, even though she was Nik's wife, she was still very much on trial. It was something he wouldn't let her forget!

Looking defiantly into his lean, speculative face, Karis felt her heartbeat quicken. He looked so harsh and sure of himself, so indestructible. What chance would anyone who opposed him have?

'That's very comforting, *agapi mou*.' If he saw her wince at the sarcastic endearment he ignored it. 'Let's hope my stay in Athens is a short one and I shall soon be able to put your assertion to the test!'

Before she had realised his intention his head bent and his hard mouth found the softness of hers, parting her lips in a deep, searching, passionate act of possession that left her gasping. Then he was brushing past her, calling for Markos as he strode towards the kitchen.

Karis slept badly that night, oddly aware of the emptiness of the bed beside her, wondering what was behind Nik's summons to Athens, and whether he would find consolation with the glamorous and successful Nikoletta. Probably if the latter had been more child-orientated they would already be man and wife! The thought gave her no comfort.

Fortunately Markos didn't appear unnecessarily perturbed by his father's absence, obviously delighting in having Karis to himself.

'We can walk right along the beach,' he told her enthusiastically over breakfast the following morning. 'Much farther than we went with Papa. There's a whole lot of rocks and little pools. Then beyond that there's another beach which goes on for ever, and there's a river without any water in it, but it's full of 'normous reeds and bamboo and we could build a shelter . . .'

'*Endaxi, endaxi* . . .!' Laughingly Karis held up her hand. 'That sounds fine by me, but I want to stay in until your Papa phones, otherwise we won't know when he'll be back.'

An hour later the phone rang.

'Ah, Karis . . .' Nik's deep voice came clearly over the

line. 'Is everything all right?'

'Yes, of course.' Impatiently she brushed his courtesies aside, her hand tightening on the receiver. 'Are you coming home today?'

'No.' Her heart sank at the uncompromising monosyllable. Somewhere in the background she heard a woman's voice raised interrogatively, followed by a silence as if Nik had covered the receiver to prevent her hearing his reply.

'Nik?' she asked sharply, her heart thudding painfully against her ribcage. 'What's happened? Can you tell me when we can expect you? Markos has been asking.'

It was a lie, but nothing would have prevailed on her to ask on her own behalf.

'A few days yet. It's Florina. She's in hospital and Giorgios won't leave her side, so I shall have to hang around until I get things organised.'

'Florina?' A pang of guilt struck Karis at her own selfish preoccupation. 'Oh, Nik—I'm so sorry . . . What's the matter?'

'Peritonitis, I'm afraid.' His voice was clipped, devoid of emotion. 'Seems like it came on entirely unexpectedly. She and my father were entertaining Nikoletta at a restaurant when suddenly Florina collapsed. Apparently it was touch and go at the time, but although she's still very ill, she's expected to make a full recovery. The trouble is it's knocked my father sideways. Before he left the restaurant in the ambulance with her he told Nikoletta to get me to take over everything—so I'm afraid I'm stuck with it.'

'Of course!' Karis's own sense of disappointment at his absence faded in the light of the news she had received. 'Please give Florina my love when you see her, and tell her and your father that they'll both be in my prayers.'

She heard his soft laugh. 'Say one for me too, will you, Karis *mou*? Ask that I'm given patience, inspiration and the ability to work twenty-four hours a day—with divine help on my side I may be able to be back at Ierapetra in two or three days' time.' Somewhere on the mainland another phone beeped and Karis heard Nik's brief farewell before she was left holding an empty line.

'Papa'll be away a day or so yet,' she told Markos, forcing her face into a false smile, 'so we'll have to amuse ourselves.'

'Is he staying with Nikoletta?' he asked innocently.

'I don't know,' she was obliged to admit. 'He's working in your grandpa's office, so I expect he'll stay in one of his hotels.'

'Grandpa doesn't like me.' It was a statement of fact, the small face showing no emotion. 'He told Papa that I wasn't his grandson and he didn't ever want to see me, that's why he never comes here.'

'Oh, darling!' Impulsively Karis bent down to hug him. 'Sometimes grown-ups get funny ideas in their heads, but as far as Papa is concerned, you are most certainly his son!'

'And yours too—now you've married him.' This time there was a question in the dark eyes to like Yanís's.

'Uh-huh,' she agreed a little breathlessly. Nik couldn't possibly object to her agreeing to that statement, could he?

'Mama wanted to go and stay with God, you know,' confided Markos, accepting the warmth of her caress without any sign of wishing to break it.

'Did she?' Karis's heart ached, wishing Nik was with them at that moment. What had Markos been told? What did he believe? Dear lord, please don't let her say the wrong thing!

The dark head nodded. 'She told me so. She said I mustn't be upset because heaven was a lovely place and she really wanted to see it, and she was just sad because Papa and I couldn't go with her yet.'

Karis blinked away her tears, still praying for the wisdom to comfort the small figure so close to her heart.

'She said when she saw God she'd ask him to send someone very special to take her place, to look after me and Papa and to love us like she had, and that we might have to wait a little time because God might not be able to find the right person straight away, but when He did we'd be happy again . . .' His voice broke off, a note of concern in his childish voice for the first time. 'Why are you crying, Karis? Didn't you want to come and look after us?'

'Of course I did!' Karis smiled through her tears. 'I'm just crying because I'm so happy. Haven't you ever felt like crying because you're so happy?'

'No.' Her son regarded her flushed face solemnly. 'I only cry when I'm sad, and not very much then, because men aren't allowed to cry when they grow up.'

'I wonder who told you that?' she murmured, remembering how Yanís had wept on that last night they had shared together. He hadn't wanted to leave his home, his family or her. Had he had a premonition that he might never return? However much it had altered the path of her life she would never regret loving him that night, turning the boy into a man, and bearing his beautiful son . . .

'Maria did.' Markos's answer surprised her. 'When I fell over and hurt my knee, but she didn't say anything to Papa when he cried after he came back from the hospital without Mama.'

'I expect he's feeling pretty miserable now as well, don't you?' With a determined effort Karis spoke cheerfully. Nik's devotion to his first wife had never been in dispute, but she was in no mood to be continually reminded of it, and the conversation was taking too morbid a turn for her liking. 'I tell you what we'll do! While he's away, you can show me all round the town and the beaches and we'll take notes, so that when Papa comes back you can show him everything we've done!'

'Great! Can we collect things too—like postcards and

seaweed and things off the beach?'

'Of course!' She found herself entering into the game with a real enthusiasm. 'We'll get Maria to give us one of those plastic carrier bags from the supermarket and we'll fill it with lovely things for Papa!'

'Great!' Markos wriggled away from her arms. 'Can we start today?'

'Why not?' She watched him scuttle from the room with a feeling of deep pride and almost unbearable affection.

During the following days Karis blessed the idea as Markos scoured the beach for things for his bag. Pieces of seaweed, the odd shell, pebbles washed smooth by the sea, pieces of glass ground down to jewel-like brilliance, a few plastic arms and legs from abandoned dolls, and the prize of the collection, a large tooth-shaped lump of ivory.

While Markos did his beachcombing she was content to sit watching him, letting the sun tan her ivory skin to a pale tan where her bikini revealed it, sometimes reading, sometimes just reliving the past, glorying in the fact that every hour strengthened the contact between herself and the child she had borne.

Only Nik remained unobtainable, his image so easily conjured before her eyes, her pulse responding to the picture caressed by her mind's eye. Nik who had suffered so much, who was bitterly opposed to his father's rejection of the child he and Andriana had nurtured, but was still loyal enough to go to his aid when requested. Or was he merely looking after his own interests? It was something she couldn't be certain about. The odds were she would never really get to know this enigmatic man, never play the part in his life that she craved.

It was the fifth day of his absence when the phone rang.

'I'll be back in Iraklion this evening. Home by ten.' Nik's clipped words made her heart sing.

'That's marvellous!' Her pleasure must have sounded

over the line.

'You sound as if you've missed me.'

'Of course we have,' her voice was more composed this time, 'but Markos has been taking good care of me . . .'

'Let me talk to him, please, Karis, please!' Beside her, her son tugged at her arm.

As she handed him the phone her face reflected her love as he gabbled out what they'd been doing, ending dramatically, 'And I've got a lovely bag of things just for you!'

The phone once more in her grip, Karis identified a note of weariness in Nik's reply as she enquired after Florina.

'She's making a splendid recovery now. Giorgios has arranged for her to recuperate at his villa on Corfu. He's engaged a whole team of medical experts to supervise her.'

'I'm glad,' she responded sincerely. Despite the Greek woman's lack of tact, she had warmed to her personality and admired her artistry. She had given up her career for Giorgios Christianides. It was good to see how much he appreciated it!

With Nik returning that evening the day seemed even brighter to Karis as she carried on with the routine they had established in his absence. By evening Markos was so tired by his exertions that despite his avowal to sit up and await Nik's return he fell asleep before eight. Looking down at his face, flushed with excitement and the kiss of the sun, as she carried him upstairs to his room, Karis felt her heart swell with joy. How lucky she was to be given this second chance!

She glanced at the gold and silver icon reproduction above the sleeping child's bed. Whoever she had to thank for what had befallen her, she would make sure she'd do her best both by her son and the man she had married, however difficult the latter might be!

It was just after ten when she heard Nik's car pull up outside the villa, and Maria's footsteps outside in the hall as she went towards the door.

'Your flight was on time, then?' It was a banal question, but it gave her time to study him as he crossed the threshold, to experience the thrill of her tightening nerves as her body responded to the sight of him. He'd been out of her life for four days, and she'd missed him like hell! How tired he looked, lines of strain round his eyes and mouth. The smile he gave her might have been for Maria's benefit, but it warmed her heart.

'Fortunately, yes,' he answered her question, stooping to give her cheek a perfunctory kiss, as Maria turned saying she was going to see if his arrival had awakened Markos. 'Did you miss me?'

'Of course,' Karis told him demurely. 'There was no one to order me around.'

'Which means that you and my son have demolished the contents of my house in my absence, does it?' He cast her a teasing look and she knew instinctively he was remembering the vision of her on the bedroom floor surrounded by broken china. 'How is he, anyway?'

'Fine, and delighted you're coming back again. He wanted to . . .'

Her sentence stopped in mid-air as there was a wail of anguish from upstairs and Maria appeared on the stairs, her face contorted with shock.

'He's gone! Markos has gone! His bed's empty and there's no sign of his shoes or the T-shirt he was wearing today. He's run away!'

'That's impossible!' Karis took the stairs two at a time, pushing the Greek woman out of her way to enter her son's room. 'He's playing a game—hiding from you! Markos! Markos! Don't play, darling! Papa's home and he wants to see you!'

Frantically she opened cupboards, looked under the bed, and found nothing. Hardly aware of Nik's presence, she rushed from room to room, a mounting dread choking her as she was forced to realise there was nowhere he could be in the streamlined bedrooms.

'I'll look downstairs.' Equally grim-faced, Nik went systematically through the ground floor rooms. Nothing.

'You had some argument? Told him off about something? Threatened him with punishment?' Nik grabbed Karis's shoulders, his face dark and distressed.

'No! How dare you blame me!' she spat at him furiously.

'I'm not blaming you, I'm trying to find a reason for this!' He fixed her with an uncompromising stare. 'For goodness sake, Karis, you must have some idea what he's up to? You've been with him for the last five days!'

'And you've been with him for the last five years!' Her voice choked with tears. 'Oh, dear heaven! Suppose he's been kidnapped!'

'Unlikely.' Nik was as emotionally disturbed as she was, struggling to keep his control and find a logical solution. 'I doubt anyone could have got in here without you or Maria hearing, and in any case kidnapping isn't a common Greek crime. Unless . . .' He paused and she saw the colour drain from his face.

'What, Nik?' She croaked her fingers digging into his arm, as she felt a wave of faintness pass over her.

'Unless you had a fancy to keep him for yourself . . .' he said slowly, his eyes like two dark accusing stars.

'You think I . . .' Horror sat starkly on Karis's ashen face. How could he possibly believe she could be so unprincipled and vicious unless he hated her with a depth of emotion that was terrifying?

She was never to know how he might have answered that question, because suddenly she remembered something that should have been in Markos's bedroom and wasn't. Something that had been there for the past couple of nights but was missing from his bedside table.

'The bag, Nik!' He looked at her as if she were mad as she shook his arms in a frenzy of excitement. 'He was collecting things to show you and keeping them in a bag. We took it out with us this afternoon on the beach, but I haven't seen it since. He must have left it there, and woken up and remembered it.'

'Dear lord!' Nik's anxiety was merited. There were no tides to worry about, of course, but at night the sea on the wild beach away from the town could become rough, sucking and swirling in the rock pools, making unexpected surges on to the dry sand. Markos could swim, but he was only a child and in the dark he could easily lose direction.

'Which way?' Nik was already at the door, his tiredness forgotten.

'To the east . . .' Karis was behind him as he sped for the front door, running in his wake as he raced down the road towards the beach, already hearing his loud deep cry as he called out their son's name.

'Papa! Papa! I found it!' The small figure emerged from the darkness to hurtle himself against Nik's legs. 'I remembered where I left it—see!' In triumph Markos held aloft the plastic bag, justifying Karis's guess, dissolving her fears. 'I woke up and it wasn't there and I thought when the man cleaned the beach early in the morning he'd take it away and . . .'

'That's enough!' Karis had never heard Nik's voice so cold. 'We'll discuss what happened when we're back home.' He hoisted Markos into his arms and, indicating that Karis should follow, turned towards the Villa Pasiphaë.

'*Tha fahs kseelo!*' Nik's hand, fingers extended and closed together as in a karate chop, gestured angrily at Markos as he dumped him unceremoniously on the floor in front of him as they all entered the main living-room.

The child's face blanched, his dark eyes seeming enormous at the threat of corporal punishment.

'But, Papa . . .' He was obviously holding back tears, unable to understand his father's fury, and Karis's heart ached for him. 'It was for you—it was your lovely bag . . .'

'Damn the bag!' Nik seized it from Markos's hand and tossed it on the floor. 'Have you any idea how much you've worried and upset . . . Karis?'

'But she knew . . .' Markos stopped as Nik made another angry, typically Greek gesture, his voice shaking with pent-up fury, the level of sound restrained out of deference to the late hour of the evening.

'You'd better get out of my sight, Markos, before I do something I may regret. We'll discuss this further in the morning.'

Karis saw the small upper lip begin to tremble and she ached for the child's distress.

'Please, Nik,' she interposed softly. 'He didn't mean to upset us. He wasn't deliberately naughty.'

'Leave this to me, please.' Nik dismissed her intercession coldly, returning his harsh gaze to the child. 'Do as I say. Go to your room.'

One brief, anguished glance in Karis's direction and Markos obeyed without another word.

'I need a brandy—and you do too!' Nik walked to the drinks cabinet as Karis watched, her eyes dwelling on his hands, seeing their nervous tremor, knowing he had been as scared as she for their son's well-being. Still the memory of that woebegone little face haunted her. Markos was only a young child, acting out of love, misguided perhaps, but wasn't that a fault she shared with him?

'I think I'll go and say goodnight to him,' she temporised as Nik turned, a glass in each hand.

'No!' he forbade her absolutely. 'Let him learn what misery feels like!'

'You're being over-harsh, Nik.' She persevered, seeking inspiration, despite the flash of anger in his dark eyes which recommended silence, and remembered something. 'When you asked me to marry you, you said a boy needed a mother to—to mediate on his behalf when his father was too stern with him . . .' Appealingly she met his hard appraisal. 'It's too much to let him lie in misery all through the night, letting him believe you hate him. Because he's too young to realise that your reaction was born of love, not hate.'

For a moment their gazes locked and Karis was sure she had lost, then Nik handed her one of the glasses and took a deep draught from the other one himself.

'You're probably right,' he conceded wearily. 'I'll have a word with him, if that'll make you happy.'

At the door he paused, re-entered the room to pick up the abandoned plastic bag and left without another word.

It was twenty minutes before he returned.

'He wants to see you now, Karis.'

'Is he all right?' There was something about the expression on Nik's face that worried her—a haunted, drawn look that tugged at her heartstrings.

'Yes, he's in top spirits.' He moved towards her, detaining her with a rough hand on her arm as she paused on the threshold. 'I've told him, Karis. Told him you are his natural mother.'

It was as shocking and unexpected as if Nik had poured a pail of icy water over her. Somehow she had anticipated that they would discuss it together first, and that Nik would be with her when Markos was told.

'Go to him. He's expecting you.' His hand moved convulsively on her arm, urging her forward.

Outside her son's door she paused, before taking a deep breath and going in.

'I guessed it! I guessed it!' He was all excitement, all joy as he stood on the bed and flung his arms round her. 'Mama will be so happy too, because God must like her lots and lots to have found you and made you love Papa. Papa says I can call you "Mummy" because that's what English children call their mothers. Papa says you only went away because you couldn't look after me and you knew Mama wanted a baby very badly and she would look after me for you, and Papa says the rocky bits we found are called quartz and the big tooth is from some old donkey . . .'

Looking at the treasures spread out on the table beside the bed, Karis's eyes filled with tears. Papa had said an awful lot in twenty minutes, and apparently never put a foot wrong—or should that be a word wrong?

'Are you crying because you're happy again?' The childish voice in her ear broke into Karis's thoughts.

'Uh-huh,' she confirmed shakily, dabbing at her eyes with a tissue. 'And because I'm glad you're safely back home.'

'I'm sorry,' Markos looked downcast. 'I promise I won't ever go out in the dark by myself again.'

She kissed the soft cheek, forgiving him the terror he had caused her, settling him down for the night before returning downstairs.

The living-room was empty, the house silent, Nik's empty brandy glass abandoned on the table. Surprised to realise how much time she had spent in Markos's bedroom, Karis finished her own drink before climbing the stairs to bed.

It was the first time Nik had preceded her there, and she had imagined he would be already asleep, tired out by his work, the journey and the traumatic events of the evening. She was wrong. He was lying on top of the bed propped up against a pillow, wearing nothing but a strip of material across his loins, his eyes fixed on the door as she entered. And he was very much awake.

CHAPTER ELEVEN

IT HAD always had to happen—the time when Nik would make their relationship into a true marriage. It was just that Karis hadn't expected it to be tonight of all nights, when both of them had already gone through so much anguish. She stood quite still inside the room, while Nik watched the expressions flitting across her countenance, his own dark face closed and unfathomable.

'There's nowhere to run to any more, *agapi mou*,' he told her softly, as lazily he swivelled his long legs off the bed. 'You're here now—home to stay.' His regard held a faint mockery as he moved across the room towards her.

Karis swallowed convulsively, every nerve of her body on edge. She wanted nothing better than to go to his arms, to feel their strength supporting her, to experience once more the hard caress of his hot, silky mouth, yet she felt frighteningly inadequate to give him the response he would demand.

If only he loved her! Perhaps in the act of love she would be able to pretend that he did, close her eyes and imagine that his demands were those of a lover rather than those of a virile man so cruelly deprived of the wife he had worshipped.

'I——' She licked her lips nervously, conscious of the dry heat of her body. 'Thank you for telling Markos the truth . . .'

'The least I could do after accusing you of spiriting him away . . .' He stood before her, overpoweringly beautiful, his skin fragrant and glowing with health, his nearness stirring her pulse to a frenzy. 'Can you forgive me?'

'For loving Markos so much?' Karis smiled up into those dark eyes, seeing and aching for their sadness. 'I could forgive you anything for that!' But his accusation *had* hurt, and now his asking for absolution pleased her.

'Then show me how you feel . . .' His hands reached out towards her, unbuttoning the shoulder straps of the pretty cotton dress she had worn to welcome him home, drawing the fabric down to reveal the simple satin cups that held her breasts.

'Oh, Nik . . .' She raised her arms, entwining them round his neck, feeling the shudder that racked his strong body, lifting her mouth to his burning kiss.

'Kardia mou, mahtia mou . . .' He breathed the words against the soft flesh of her cheek, as his urgent hands found and released the catch on her bra.

My heart, my eyes . . . those were the words he had used. How could she not respond to them? Forget Andriana, forget Nikoletta . . . Believe that it was she, Karis, whom he loved. With shaking hands she discarded her own bra, offering her breasts to Nik's questing mouth, arching her body against his bare skin, feeling the surge of his manhood and revelling in it.

There was no need for words as Nik's eyes, dazed and dreamy, gazed on her revealed flesh with such naked desire that Karis's spirit leapt.

Obeying his silent command, she separated herself from the delicate feminine garments that had hidden her from his gaze, feeling a surge of exultation at the expression on his face. It would be all right. It *had* to be all right.

'Dear lord, but you're exquisite!' He stared at her nakedness like a pilgrim before a shrine, as a thrill of expectation flowed through her veins. 'I've waited so long to enjoy you, Karis *mou* . . .' His arms enfolded her, drawing her to his near-naked body, moulding her against him curve to hollow, as his mouth traced a passage of fire on her forehead, moving to her cheek, before it captured her soft lips.

He took her mouth with all the force of a predator who knew he would not be challenged, and Karis welcomed him, with the resignation of a prey whose destiny was already known and accepted, drawing his tongue into the dark cavity of her own mouth, caressing it, welcoming its intrusion, every fibre of her body wanting to merge with Nik, to be possessed by him. Never to be alone again. Never to have to face life as half a person. To be part of a greater entity, to be one with the man she loved as she had never known love before. To possess and be possessed by Nikolaos Christianides. That had always been her destiny, and now she recognised the fact with a great joy and mounting excitement.

When he lifted her into his arms, she clung to him. When he laid her gently on the bed, she smiled up at him. When he stripped himself naked and came to her, she truly thought she was ready for him.

He didn't speak as he lowered himself over her, covering her body with his own. Hard and seeking, he presented himself at the door to paradise—and was rejected.

Karis had turned to ice. Heaven alone knew how she desired him, how desperately she wanted to give him the release he sought, yet the message from her brain seemed to have been diverted. Perhaps it was the memory of the first, the only time she had been possessed by a man that had returned to haunt her, but her muscles had tautened, rejecting the threat of invasion.

Desperately she tried to relax, offering herself to the man she loved, but finding it impossible to overcome the defence her body had mounted against an invader. Useless to tell herself that Nik wasn't some immature, inexperienced lover who would hurt her as Yanís had done unwittingly all those years ago. Useless to tell herself that he would be gentle and understanding, because the warm, erotic scent of his arousal denied it, as did every surge of his virile body.

He would force past her defences, unknowing or uncaring of the trauma he would cause, and she would bear the pain because, despite the evidence of her tissues, she wanted him. Wanted him to take her, to make her part of his life and his future.

Even while she fought with her own body's hostility, bracing herself for the ultimate invasion, she heard his moan of disbelief, the swallowed imprecation. Unbelieving, she felt the cool evening air against her nakedness as he rolled away and knew she was losing him. Not just for now, but perhaps for ever . . .

'Nik!' She cried out his name, too distraught to be embarrassed. 'Nik, don't leave me!'

'Karis . . .' Her name was thick on his tongue. 'Karis . . . you *are* my wife, you *are* Markos's mother. You have no need to prove it.'

'But I want to!' She reached out despairingly, her fingers latching round his arm as he would have risen from the bed.

'You don't want me.' The flat statement called her a liar, and she knew she must explain, tell him what she wanted . . . what she needed . . . and why.

'Nik!' she beseeched. 'Please listen to me. I'm not as experienced as you think. Yanís . . .' She felt him flinch but continued doggedly. 'It was just the once. He . . . we . . .' She stumbled over the words, but knew it was vital to make Nik understand. 'We were both young, inexperienced. He didn't mean to hurt me, but neither of us understood . . .'

'Once?' He was motionless now, only his dark questioning eyes narrowed in shock, moving to wash across her strained face. 'And it was bad for you?'

She nodded, unable to condemn in words the young Greek who, caught in the throes of his own passion, had been blind to her discomfort.

'I see.' His dark gaze caressed her. 'You need more time . . .'

'Yes—no . . .' she contradicted herself in her agony to make him understand that the time she needed could be measured in minutes, not weeks. She recalled his firm capable hands, their gentleness and strength as he had held Markos. She wanted to feel those hands on her own body, teasing, cajoling, driving away the icy rigidity which had frozen her muscles.

'I—what I really want, Nik, is for you to—to make love to me.' Her voice broke. 'Now, this moment, I want you to make love to me—not just take me!'

'Make love to you!' In the dimly lit room she could still make out the astonishment on his lean features, hear the rough bark of laughter in his throat. 'If you only knew what you were asking!'

She had no hold on him now, watching in dismay as he rose to his feet, shrugging a short silk robe over his shoulders. She had lost him after all. In demanding the intimacies of a devoted lover she had reminded him that she was only second best. An icy shiver trembled from her head to her toes as she turned to bury her face in the soft pillows as he moved away, shuddering as she heard the bedroom door close behind him.

Now when she most needed them she was denied the comfort of tears, left destitute and dry-eyed to curse the contrariness of her wayward flesh.

'Karis?' She hadn't heard Nik return. Reluctantly she opened her eyes and blinked. There, on a level with her gaze, held in the firm hand she knew so well, was a glass foaming with what could only be champagne.

Struggling upwards, she met Nik's dark regard.

'You wanted me to love you.' There was a smile in his dark voice which promised her unspoken pleasures. 'This is just the beginning!'

The beginning of a journey into a world of sensual pleasures as her full capabilities of adoring and being adored were discovered and cultivated as she was about to realise. For Nik loved her slowly, oh, so slowly, with reverence and passion, as she had prayed he might, finding her natural rhythm and going along with it, masterfully conjuring up chords of response she had never known herself capable of feeling, orchestrating her emotions until beneath his skilled tuition they burst forth into a wild concerto of love and longing.

When the time came for him to take her for his own, her body had long since ceased to raise barriers against him. Every sense clamouring for his possession, it was Karis herself who begged for Nik's dominion, exulting in the final act of consummation. Accepting the culmination of the night's pleasure as her triumph and fulfilment.

There was no need to ask Nik if it had been good for him. She knew intuitively that he had journeyed with her, tempering his spiral of arousal to the slower ascent of her own, but reaching the climax with her, spilling his life force into her at the moment she had reached her own paradise. Trembling and weak, their breaths mingling, their flesh damp and satiated, they clung together waiting for the calm to follow the storm.

When her breathing had returned to normal Karis eased herself slightly, escaping the half-weight of Nik's lethargic body as it lay against her. His slow even breathing proclaimed him asleep, the sudden calming unconsciousness that so often followed the excitement and energy of total fulfilment.

Tonight he had given her everything she had wanted. Everything, with the exception of his undying love, and she wasn't stupid enough or selfish enough to demand that. There had been no need or time for words between them, but deep inside her she felt the need to record the wealth of love she felt for the man she had married.

Raising herself on one elbow, reaching out towards one of the abandoned champagne glasses, she discerned a mouthful of wine still in its bowl. Smiling to herself in the darkness, she dipped her forefinger into the liquid. Carefully, so as not to disturb him, she leant over Nik's tanned, silky back, her hand trembling slightly on the taut golden skin as she inscribed in Greek script the words she had been too diffident to speak. *S'agapo, agapi mou*, she wrote. *S'agapo!*

The sun was slanting strongly through the blinds when she awakened the following morning to find the bed beside her empty. Karis stretched luxuriously, her fingers smoothing the sheet beside her where Nik's body had lain in satisfied slumber. Last night he had demonstrated to her how a loving, caring man could make the act of love a supreme experience for a woman and every cell of her body exulted in that knowledge. He might never love her as he had loved Andriana, but if he cared enough to give her the pleasure she had craved from him so generously, their future life together might be happier than she had dared to hope when she had first undertaken the responsibility of marriage.

A sound at the bedroom door had her drawing the crumpled sheet over her nudity in case it was Markos coming in for a cuddle. Instead it was Nik himself who appeared on the threshold, carrying a tray.

'I thought we'd have breakfast in here this morning.' His tone was coolly impersonal as he set the tray down beside her before going to the windows and allowing more light into the room. As he turned she could see that he had showered and shaved, although he still wore the short silk robe beneath which his bare legs suggested he had little else on.

'Lovely!' They could have been two strangers instead of a man and a woman who had shared a night of glorious, intimate passion. Karis pushed herself upright, lifting the sheet with her to cover her breasts while she searched for the nightdress which should have been under the pillow.

Her head turned, she hadn't realised Nik's proximity until the sheet was twitched out of her fingers. 'Not after last night, Karis *mou*.' His dark eyes glinted with amusement. 'Your modesty is charming but unnecessary, *né?*'

'I thought Markos might join us,' she riposted quickly, but that hadn't been the whole reason. At the back of her mind had been the thought that in the cool light of the morning, his desire assuaged, Nik might not relish the sight of her nakedness. Clearly she had been wrong, and her mistake gave her a warm glow of pleasure, as she made no effort to replace the sheet.

'Markos and Maria aren't here,' he told her blandly, smiling as her eyes widened in surprise and she asked,

'They've gone out already? But the shops aren't open yet . . .'

'Have you forgotten the date?' Then as he saw her puzzled look. 'I see you have. It's May Day, so Maria and Markos have gone out to gather their flowers from the fields before they wilt in the heat, and afterwards they're going on to visit Tonia's parents.'

'Oh, I would have liked to go with them!' She had always thought the Greek custom of picking flowers on May Day and taking them home to make lucky wreaths to hang on the front doors of the houses was a charming one—in direct contrast to the parade of heavy tanks and guns with which some other countries saw fit to celebrate the beginning of spring.

Nik looked at her with amused surprise. 'Then you and I will go out together later in the day and pick flowers, if that's what you wish.' Solemnly he poured her out a cup of coffee. 'But first I think we need to talk.'

'Must we?' Karis took a sip of the coffee, refusing to meet his eyes. The last thing she wanted was a post-mortem on what had happened between them, and instinct told her that

Nik was about to demolish the fantasies she had allowed herself to enjoy in his arms—fantasies of their sharing a true, reciprocal love.

'Listen to me, Karis.' Firmly he took the cup from her hand. 'Last night while I was lying half asleep, dreaming that perhaps in time I would be able to make you love me a tenth of the amount you must have loved Markos's father, I imagined I felt someone writing on my back.' He paused as she lifted her clear, light eyes to stare in wonder at his serious face.

Even the fact that he had detected her schoolgirlish graffiti was insignificant in the light of what he had just told her. He had hoped she would be able to love him? He cared enough about her to want her love? And a tenth of the amount she'd felt for Yanís! He would be satisfied with that! He must be teasing her . . .

As doubt clouded her eyes, Nik lifted her hands in his own, and there was no amusement now in his expression. 'Did I imagine it, *kardia mou*?' he asked her softly, his voice oddly husky. 'Or do you love me?''

He had called her 'my heart', as if she were truly a part of his body, and for a brief second as she saw the strong pulse in his throat beat and felt her own heart thud in unison Karis felt she was. His glance caressed the tumble of her chestnut curls and came to rest on her slightly parted lips as if willing the response he desired. Stomach muscles tensed, she looked into his dark, handsome face, guessing that the answer was already written across her countenance and that lying to save her pride would be cowardly as well as futile.

'Yes,' she told him helplessly, and then, because confession was a balm to her aching spirit, 'More than I've ever loved any man in my whole life.'

'Even Yanís?' The question came swiftly and harshly, as if he hated to ask it.

'Differently,' she averred truthfully. 'And yes—in so

many more dimensions . . .' She raised one of his hands to her face, resting her cheek against it, closing her eyes, enjoying the brush of his skin against her own, believing she understood what was behind his catechism. Remorseful because he had wrongly suspected her of spiriting Markos away, Nik had told her son her true identity before he had intended to, before she had passed the tests he had no doubt set her. It was important to him now that she would keep faith.

She heard his shuddering sigh just seconds before she felt the warm salute of his lips against the tender summit of one of her exposed breasts. Her sharp, responsive exclamation was buried in the crisp darkness of his hair as she rested her face in its dark luxuriance, fighting against the wicked thrill of anticipation that tingled through her receptive body.

'It was bad enough when I believed you'd had a dozen lovers . . .' His voice was muffled as he turned his head against her and she held him there, clasping his silk-clad shoulders, feeling the erotic touch of the material against her bare skin and thinking how much more erotic it would have felt if it had been the hot satin of his nakedness. 'But when you told me the truth—how there had been only one man in your life . . .' He pushed himself away from her to stare down at her with agonised eyes. 'It was then I truly knew the bitter pain of jealousy. I might have won you from an unfaithful lover—but how could I hope to compete with a dead one?'

How indeed? But if he realised the irony of his statement he was showing no sign of it. Karis expelled her breath in a long sigh. She had admitted too much to withdraw now. If Nik needed total evidence of her capitulation he should have it.

'We were both very young,' she told him quietly. 'Yanís was a lovely man—kind, considerate, fun to be with. He offered me all the affection I so desperately needed—it was inevitable I should love him first as a friend and then as someone I thought I could share my life with . . .'

'But not for eternity?' Nik interjected harshly as she paused. 'Is that what you're saying, Karis? That if he'd lived you might not have been happy together?'

'How can I answer that?' Suddenly she was angry. How dared Nik want his pound of flesh and blood as well! But he had read her thoughts accurately and she shivered at his perception.

'Forgive me!' He was quick to repentance. 'Goodness knows I have no right to question you, but you've been a part of my life for so long, I forget you're not answerable to me.'

'So long?' There was more here than she understood: much more. Nik's face was taut with hard-held emotion, his voice low and intense as he held her troubled gaze with steady scrutiny.

'The first time I saw you I wanted you,' he said bleakly, ignoring her gasp of shock. 'Yes, wanted you, Karis *mou*.' His eyes were brilliant with remembered pain. 'I was happily married, contented . . . and the revelation was shocking and distasteful.'

How clearly she remembered that first meeting—his coolness, his impertinent dismissal of her presence. 'Go on,' she murmured, fascinated by this insight into his true reactions, yet unbearably hurt by his obvious contempt.

Nik gave her a reluctant smile. 'I'm not a superstitious man, but I felt strongly that our future lives would be entwined, and I fought that premonition as hard as I could, because there could be nothing between us without injuring Andriana . . .' he paused as she saw the sorrow soften and darken the luminosity of his eyes '. . . and I loved my wife.'

'I know.' The pale torment of his face shocked her, and she could feel the anguish within him, longed to alleviate it, yet dreaded to add to his pain. 'Oh, Nik, I don't expect to

replace Andriana in your heart or your life . . .' She stopped
as a bitter tightness constricted her throat. All she wanted
was to occupy some corner of his heart, but the lump in her
throat vied with her pride to make the admission impossible.

'Darling—don't!' Nik gathered her to him, pressing her
unashamed flesh hard against him, cradling her head against
his shoulder as his hands threaded through her hair. 'I'm
trying to tell you that I do love you, that I knew it from the
first time I saw you. I tried to fight it because I could see no
future for it . . . It was as if the gods were taunting me with
your image, tantalising me with the impossibility of ever
possessing you. The day we spent together on the beach was
meant to bring me back to my senses, but it had just the
opposite effect, leaving me feeling frustrated and guilty as
hell!'

He gave a bitter laugh as, too astounded to interrupt,
Karis savoured the aromatic animal warmth of his skin,
drawing comfort from his nearness as she tried to assimilate
his torrent of words. Nik loved her? 'That Christmas when I
came to the hotel and discovered you were pregnant, I was
devastated. I felt as if you'd betrayed me!'

'But, Nik . . .' she protested, lifting her head and seeing
the pain twisting across his lean face.

'I know—it was insane.' His avid gaze devoured her.
'But there was no way I could deny it. In a strange way I felt
it should be my child you were carrying, and I knew I had to
do everything possible to ensure you came to no harm.'

'It was you!' Suddenly she understood what had puzzled
her at the time but she had long since passed to the back of
her mind. 'There was no charitable trust at the hospital! It
was you who paid for my treatment. Your money which
saved Markos's life!' Her breath sawed harshly as she
realised just how important his intervention had been.

'It was something I had to do,' he admitted quietly. 'The
hospital itself was sworn to secrecy, but when you decided to

have Markos adopted there was only one home to which he could logically have come. One home which already had love waiting for him. For some time Andriana and I had talked about adopting, and she was thrilled at the idea.'

'But did she . . .' Karis blanched as an idea struck her. How had his wife coped with her childlessness and Nik's preoccupation with a foreigner's offspring? 'Nik—did your wife think you were my lover?'

'No, *agapi mou*.' He smiled at her anguish. 'Andriana never knew how I felt about you, but she did know I was never unfaithful to her, that I respected her too much to hurt her that way. To understand our relationship you need to know how it came about. We'd known each other for many years, you see, since she was ten and I twelve. We were friends and confidants long before we became husband and wife. Andriana was my second cousin—my father's cousin's daughter. When her parents were killed in a hotel fire in the States Giorgios offered her a home here in Greece.'

His eyes were on Karis's still face, but his gaze was introverted, stretching back into the past. All she could do was lie quiescent in his arms and listen. 'She was in a state of shock, orphaned, transported from the only country she had ever known, with not very much Greek to help her to communicate. I was still suffering from the tragic, unexpected death of my own mother . . . We found solace together. I helped her with her Greek and she——' his eyelids blinked the lashes resting on his cheeks for a second longer than necessary, 'she let me cry on her shoulder and never told a living soul.'

Still unable to find the right words, Karis contented herself with lifting one hand and stroking Nik's smooth jaw, feeling the tension relax beneath her gentle caress.

'Ah, well . . .' He took her hand, pressed it palm open to his lips for a brief second, accepting her compassion, before keeping her fingers imprisoned in his own grasp. 'You can see how strong was the bond which developed between us—and Giorgios encouraged us to be interested in each other. In fact, it was his assumption that we would eventually marry that made us first consider the idea.'

'You didn't actually fall in love with her, then?' she ventured.

'No,' Nik agreed quietly. 'But I didn't realise that at the time, because it wasn't an emotion I had ever experienced. Desire—yes, as is natural to all young men as they grow up, but even in that respect Andriana was different. I'd always thought of her more as a sister than a lover.' He paused and a harder note deepened his voice as he continued. 'Later I realised that Giorgios's urgency in promoting the marriage was to ensure that Andriana's twenty-six-per-cent holding in the company didn't fall into alien hands.'

'But you were happy together?' Karis broke his reverie and he gave her a sad smile.

'Yes, we were happy, or perhaps contented is a better word. Life continued very much the same for us after the wedding as before. Andriana—Andriana was never very strong, she tired easily, and because I cared for her I accepted that her greatest pleasures were in home-making and the gentler domestic duties so many of today's women turn their backs on. As you already know, she desperately wanted a family, and when we found out that was impossible she was distraught for several months. In fact she had so much difficulty in sleeping that I agreed to her request to have separate beds. Eventually she did improve, but by then we had got used to sleeping apart, and since there was no possibility of children from our union Andriana lost all interest in making love.'

'And you still remained faithful!' Somehow it was difficult to imagine Nik living a celibate life. He was one of the most masculine men Karis had ever met, and last night she had discovered him capable of seemingly limitless passion.

'After seeing what effect my father's infidelity had on my mother, what choice did I have?' Nik asked harshly. 'Besides, sex without love is a fleeting pleasure. I told you, I cared for Andriana, loved her as another human being, and she loved and trusted me. On our wedding day she had made over all her shareholding to me. That was the extent of her trust. I could never have abused it!'

'Yet your father still expected you to divorce her?' Karis asked, astounded.

'He was obsessed with founding his own dynasty.' His fingers trailed gently down her bare arm. 'So much so that when we adopted Markos he took it as a personal affront, accused me of trying to cheat him of heirs—but you already know all that.'

'Yes. And now,' Karis murmured halfway between a smile and a sob, 'it looks as if he might get his own way after all.'

'He must do whatever he wishes, because I shall never disinherit Markos,' Nik said stubbornly. 'Whatever Giorgios does I shall always see that Markos is on equal terms. Tell me, Karis . . . do you still believe I meant to tell him I was the boy's natural father?'

The question took her by surprise. How could she, after what he had just told her? But in that hotel room in Iraklion she had had no idea of the part she had already played in his life, even now she was having difficulty in convincing herself that he loved her.

'You didn't deny it,' she said at last.

'Because I was angry that you could even consider I could have been so devious and insensitive,' he admitted wryly. 'Besides, I wanted to make love to you very much. It seemed a good way to gain your co-operation and persuade you to overcome your revulsion to me.'

'I was never revolted.' Karis smiled reminiscently, remembering the scene in London when she had given him that impression. 'In fact, I was shocked at the way you could make me want you when I'd already decided there was no room for another man in my life.'

'Could I?' His fingertips were still taking pleasure from the smooth warm skin of her arm. 'I was blind to such knowledge. For five years I'd loved Markos, watched him grow and thrive, been painfully aware of how much he resembled you in looks. With Markos as my son it was impossible to forget you, try as I might. You were always there in his laughter and his tears.'

'Nik . . .' She breathed his name as his fingers tightened around her arm, a little scared by his vehemence.

'I loved your son, Karis—and through him my feelings for you had matured. I'd always known that what I felt for you in those early days had had to be based on more than just desire, because I was strong enough to control my desires, yet what I felt for you refused to be controlled—it continued to haunt me through my marriage and beyond . . . and then I came to London, knowing that the time had come for me to remarry and give Markos the mother he deserved, and there you were . . .'

He stopped speaking to kiss her, possessing her mouth with a burning urgency, before continuing. 'Can you imagine how I felt? It was an agonising decision for me to make. If you were the promiscuous flirt everyone thought you, dared I offer you charge of your son? Shouldn't his interests come first? Yet I was burning to take you in my arms, crush the life out of you, make you pay for your sins because you'd never sinned with me! I couldn't let you escape me this time because I was free to take you as the gods had always intended, but I had to know the cost . . .'

'Nik—stop it, please stop it!'

He'd baited her in London, forced her to reveal her pain and it had hurt, but now she understood she could forgive him everything. His arms tightened round her, crushing her, hurting her as the last barriers he had erected against his own nature came tumbling down.

They were two of a kind. Karis knew it as her flesh quickened and her loins burned in silent invitation. She too had shut herself away from the physical expression of love, denied by a loveless childhood in the same way as Nik himself, and afterwards by the strength of her own self-control. Now she knew he was right. They had always been intended to meet and join, become one flesh.

Nik was caressing her—drawing his fine hands down her body, cupping her breasts, anointing them with his mouth with a delicate eagerness as she pushed the robe from his broad shoulders, reaching to unknot its tie and sighing with satisfaction as it slid to the floor.

'Last night when you asked me to make love to you, it was the culmination of all my dreams—all my hopes. You see, it was never going to be enough for you to just accept me. Unless you came to me willingly it would be rape . . . and I could never have hurt you that way,' he murmured against her skin. 'I'd meant to wait until you'd settled down, try to court you, make you see I wasn't the unfeeling brute I'd appeared to be, but the shock of Markos's disappearance . . .'

'Don't remind me!' Last night Nik had taught her how to please him and she had learned the lesson well, hearing his gasp of pleasure as she caressed him.

'It was worse for me.' His voice was shaky, scarcely controlled. 'Because if I'd lost Markos, I would have lost you too.'

'No, oh no!' Karis denied his surmise with agitation. 'Didn't you realise I could never leave you?'

'Not until you begged me to love you—and not even then, perhaps . . .' He was drawing the words out with difficulty, his voice heavy and hoarse. 'Not until I felt the words you wrote burning into my flesh—and I dared to believe . . .'

'Believe, believe,' Karis crooned. *'S'agapo, agapi mou, s'agapo.'*

'Kardia mou . . . mahtia mou . . .' The sweet words of possession jerked from Nik's lips as he thrust the remaining fragment of sheet from between their seeking bodies. *S'agapo,* Karis *mou, s'agapo . . .'*

They were the last words spoken for a very long while, as the coffee grew cold in its pot beside them . . .

EPILOGUE

POSITIVE! Karis murmured her thanks and replaced the receiver on its rest. Tonight when Nik got home from Iraklion she would cook him a special meal, send Maria out for the evening and break the news to him that he was going to become a father in about seven months' time! It would be a fitting addition to their present happiness, a widening of their closely knit family circle. She would have to be particularly careful Markos wouldn't feel left out of things during the first few hectic days after the newcomer's arrival, but her son was a remarkably well-adjusted child, happy and expansive in the warm blanket of love which surrounded him.

The doorbell rang, interrupting her musing. Surely Markos and Maria weren't back from their shopping expedition already? Automatically she ran her fingers through her hair, checking her appearance in the hall mirror and grinning at her own radiant reflection, before obeying the summons.

Giorgios Christianides stood on the threshold.

'Nik!' Her first thought was that something had happened to the man she loved and his father had come to tell her personally. Why else would Nik's father come to the house he had sworn never to set foot in until his son presented him with a true heir? Devious and cunning the elder Christianides might be, but he could hardly know what she herself had only discovered a few seconds ago!

'Still in Iraklion, if he's doing the job he's paid for!' Giorgios said gruffly. 'I haven't come to see him. I've come to see you—and my grandson.'

'Your grandson?' Karis stared at him in bewilderment. 'You mean Markos?'

'He's the only grandson I've got, isn't he?' Eyes as black as Nik's glared at her. 'Am I welcome here or not?'

'Of course.' Blushing at her lack of courtesy, she stood back, inviting him to enter. 'It's just that I thought . . . I mean . . .' she floundered helplessly as her father-in-law walked past her into the sunlit sitting-room. Did this mean that Giorgios was actually acknowledging Markos's right to bear the family name after all this time? 'What I mean to say is that Markos and Maria are out together, but I'm expecting them back soon.'

Did Nik know he was here? Somehow she thought not, but it was the first time since his name-day party that she had seen Giorgios Christianides, and she was very aware of his commanding aura that didn't invite questions.

'May I offer you a drink while you're waiting?' she asked politely, relieved when he nodded and she saw traces of a smile on his stern mouth.

'Ouzo on ice, please.'

A traditional drink for a traditional man, Karis thought, listening to the sharp crack of the ice as she poured the liquid over it.

'Has Nik mentioned to you this idea Nikoletta's had?' he asked abruptly as he accepted the glass from her with a sharp nod of thanks.

'No.' She slid open the large patio door which gave access to the garden, allowing the warm July breeze to circulate round the room, before seating herself demurely opposite her visitor.

He made an expansive movement with his free hand. 'She intends to add a line of jewellery to her fashion boutiques and thought you might be interested in advising her, putting her in touch with designers—perhaps formulating some of your own ideas.'

'I'd love to!' Eagerly she leant forward, clasping her hands between her knees. Even with a baby on the way it was something she could do with pleasure and fulfilment. 'Can you tell me more?'

'No, I'm sorry . . .' To her astonishment her father-in-law actually looked embarrassed. 'I shouldn't have mentioned it anyway. Nik's the one with all the details. He probably wanted to tell you himself. He seemed to think you'd jump at the idea.'

'Well, I won't say anything until he does, then.' Karis took a deep breath, sensing there was another reason for the older man's presence, and one he was finding difficulty in broaching. 'Is there something else you wanted to tell me?'

Giorgios emptied the glass of ouzo in one large swallow, put the empty tumbler on the table and thrust himself to his feet. 'Florina and I are getting married!' he said baldly, and walked towards the open door, turning his back towards her.

'But that's wonderful!' Karis cried, and meant it.

'She thinks so.' Giorgios turned and the dark humour in his eyes reminded her of Nik. 'The truth of the matter is, I didn't realise how much she meant to me until I nearly lost her. I'm not a young man any more and I want to grow old with my family around me. It's something I've only just realised.' He smiled at her, a wry self-deprecating smile that stirred her compassion. 'In the event Florina will have a life interest in my estates, after that everything goes to Nik to do with as he pleases.'

'He doesn't want your money—neither of us does.' She hoped desperately he wouldn't think she was being ungracious.

'I know that!' he told her gruffly. 'But where else should it go if not to the family—all the family?'

'Has Nik told you . . .' Karis paused delicately, trying to choose the right words, but she was pre-empted.

'That you're Markos's natural mother? Yes.' Giorgios

nodded as she sighed her relief. She and Nik had agreed the fact would be allowed to emerge naturally and she was glad Giorgios had become one of the first to know.

'He also told me his father was a brave young man, killed in the service of Greece.' He fixed her with his magnetic eyes. 'Any man would be proud to acknowledge a heritage like that in his grandson!'

'Thank you.' It was all she could say.

'I knew Nik had found the right wife as soon as I saw you,' the deep voice continued thoughtfully. 'Andriana was a gentle, pretty girl, but she was no match for my son's fire and enthusiasm—but there were reasons . . .' His voice tailed away before he added briskly, 'At least she was happy while the marriage lasted, but when I saw you wearing Irene's sapphires . . .' He gestured explicitly with both hands. 'I expect you realised they were the most public declaration of his feelings for you that Nik could make.'

Then she hadn't. Now she did. 'Yes,' she whispered.

Fortunately, because she hadn't wanted to allow her overwrought emotions to manifest themselves in a flood of tears, the sound of Maria's key in the door, accompanied by Markos's chatter, proved a welcome diversion.

'Mummy! Mummy!' Her son came bounding into the room. 'We've been to the fish market and we've got *calamari* and a lobster, and Maria . . .' He froze as the tall bulky figure at the window moved a few steps into the room.

'Markos, this is your grandpa.' Her heart thudding like a captured bird, Karis made the introduction, conscious of Maria's astonished silence in the background. 'He's come all the way from Athens just to see you.'

'Grandpa?' Markos frowned, raising hesitant innocent eyes to the tall form before him, while Karis prayed he would be given the gift of tact.

'Have you got a hug for me?' Giorgios sank to his knees, holding out his arms. To a child raised to affection the gesture was irrefusable.

'Do you like *calamari*, Grandpa?' Locked in Giorgios's arms, his soft cheek against the hard skin of the older man, Markos whispered his question.

'Of course!' Giorgios sounded shocked. 'Doesn't everyone?'

'Kyrios Christianides will be staying for lunch and dinner,' smoothly Karis instructed Maria, a patina of calm crusting the buoyant thrust of excitement that thrilled every nerve in her body. 'I'm expecting Kyrios Nikolaos home early this evening. While Markos and his grandpa are getting to know each other I'll come and help you in the kitchen.' She smiled conspiratorially at the Greek woman. 'Tonight we must make a very special meal—there's so much we have to celebrate!'

'*Né*, Kyria Karis . . .' It was the first time Maria had ever used her Christian name, the first time she had ever smiled at her with unremitting approval. '*Né*, Kyria Karis . . . tonight we have a celebration like none the Villa Pasiphaë has ever seen!'

Six exciting series for you every month... from Harlequin

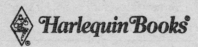

HARLEQUIN

Romance®

Delight in the exotic yet innocent love stories of
Harlequin Romance.

Be whisked away to dazzling international capitals ... or
quaint European villages.

Experience the joys of falling in love ... for the first
time, the best time!

Six new titles every month for your
reading enjoyment!

HRG-1